# JACE

## RIVER PACK WOLVES 2

### ALISA WOODS

October 2015 Edition
Sworn Secrets Publishing

Cover Design by Steven Novak

ISBN-13: 978-1545299494
ISBN-10: 1545299498

### Jace (River Pack Wolves 2)
### His wolf is out of control.
### She's a wild thing that won't be tamed.

Ex-Army Specialist Jace River has a lock on his bedroom door, but it's not to keep anyone out; it's to keep his nightmares from breaking loose. His wolf is an out-of-control killer, which means he can never risk shifting, never truly be part of his pack, and definitely never take a mate.

Piper Wilding works for the Army as a civilian, traveling the world for her work in counterintelligence and fighting the bad guys while bedding down the good ones. The best part? It keeps her far from her asshole father in Seattle, the rest of the Wilding pack, and the pressure to take a mate. Settling down isn't her thing, and after what happened to her mother, Piper vowed she would never be tied down by magic or men again.

While Jace's wolf keeps him Sleepless in Seattle, Piper returns home to find her missing kid brother. When she breaks into the River brothers' safehouse, sparks fly and claws come out. Her sexy skills threaten to bring out Jace's wolf, and Jace's good-guy hotness reminds Piper how tempting shifter men can be. They're like fire and gasoline, and as they race to find Piper's brother, the heat threatens to burn down all their carefully constructed walls. But falling in love has never been so dangerous—and being together means taking risks that neither might survive.

# CHAPTER 1

The flames singe his fur. The screams tear through his soul. But Jace's beast is wild, uncontrollable, and rampaging through the falling embers of the tiny village. He tries to hold his wolf back, but it dives through a wall of fire to the cowering people inside. The hut is an inferno, and the husband and wife are trapped. His wolf snarls and lunges at them, ramping their screams even higher… somehow, Jace wrestles his beast away from clamping down on their flailing arms and exposed necks. Then a cry breaks through the crackling heat—a child. His wolf hungers to go after *the plaintive sound; Jace fights to stop it, but the beast is too strong. It scents the child's raspberry smell through the acrid smoke and dashes after her. It crashes through a corrugated wall like a demon, the flimsy construction no obstacle for a wolf like him—twice the size of any normal shifter and unleashed from human control.*

*The girl shrieks when it finds her. She clutches her doll tighter and shrinks into the corner, covering the stringy black hair on her head with a tiny hand. His beast roars and lunges for her, fangs bared—*

Jace heaved upright in his bed, panting and fighting to keep from shifting. To keep the beast contained within his body and his dream. His claws were embedded in the mattress—he had ripped long slashes deep into the stuffing, and his blankets were a nest of shredded linen. He gritted his teeth and growled as he forced the claws to retract. *Too close.*

"Fuck," he breathed out, rubbing his face with his now-human hands. The moonlight spilled into his bedroom, giving just enough glow to see the door—still locked. He had triple locks installed on his apartment in the city, but here at his family's estate, he'd only been able to talk his mother into installing one. She didn't understand, didn't know what he turned into when the nightmare got hold of him. She was a shifter, too, but she had her wolf under control... like every other normal person.

Jace's wolf had always been freakishly strong—twice the size of his brothers, flipping unbelievable in strength, and always a little on the wild side. Even as a pup, he had to work to get his beast to obey his human thoughts—to *belong* to him, like every other shifter seemed to manage with ease. Then Jace went overseas with the Army and served his country like he had always dreamed of doing... and something happened. He lost it. Lost control. *Became* the beast.

And people paid for it with their lives.

A shudder gripped him, and Jace forced himself to breathe out the last of the nightmare from his system. That was the quickest way to bury the beast deep inside again. The nightmare always brought it out, as if by reliving the scene over and over, he could change the past. But he couldn't. He could never right that wrong... but he should be able to keep his beast under control while staying in his mother's house, for fuck's sake. If not, he might have to go back to the city, something he didn't want to do. Not until he and his brothers, Jaxson and Jared, had caught up with this Agent Smith character. They'd given him an ass-kicking, and he was on the run, but he'd been kidnapping shifters straight off the streets of Seattle and performing some kind of medical experiments on them. The River pack had rescued a bunch of shifters, but who knew how many Agent Smith still had tucked away in some dungeon?

That shit had to stop.

Jace would just have to keep things under control while they figured out their next move.

He glanced at the clock. *3 am.* Too early to get up, but there wouldn't be any more sleep for him for the rest of the night anyway. Not that he wanted to—slipping back into the nightmare was all too easy once his dream wolf had already been unleashed.

Jace stretched the aches of his muscles, still cramped from fighting the shift, and swung his legs out of bed. His sleep pants had avoided the shredding, and the warm summer air meant he'd forgone a t-shirt, but the bed was a mess. He sighed and tossed the comforter over the torn bedding. He'd have to fix that later. For now, he needed some chow. Something to eat would wake him up, reset the clock, and hopefully get him through another day.

Until he had to face the night again.

The estate was huge—two dozen bedrooms, a massive front room and dining area, enormous kitchen. And that was just in the main house. Out the back, nestled against the Washington mountainside with the stables, there were even more cabins… one with his brother Jaxson no doubt having the time of his life with his new mate, Olivia. She'd come into their lives like a whirlwind, but somehow she'd figured out his brother's secret and set him free from it… all without Jace knowing until it was all over. Jaxson had always been there for him, ever since he'd been discharged from the Army, but he'd completely failed to be there in return. Jace hadn't even known something was wrong, too busy dealing with his own problems or chasing after bad guys to try to forget them. He should have known Jaxson was carrying a darkness around inside him. Just another thing Jace's wolf managed to fuck up in his life.

Jace quietly unlocked his bedroom door and crept down the stairs, keeping his footfalls silent as he worked his way toward the kitchen. He didn't need his problems to wake up everyone else. His mom had been taking in wayward shifters for a while, ever since their dad died, and there was always someone staying at the safehouse who wasn't actually a member of the River family. Right now, the place was full-up, with most of the River brothers' pack doubling up in the rooms and filling every available bed. They even had a few from the Wilding pack staying with them, not to mention the shifter prisoners they had just broken free from Agent Smith's torturous grasp.

Even with a full house, the place was silent, except for the occasional creak of the log construction, the squeak of the stairs as he descended, and the whisper of the pines outside. He'd always loved that sound as a kid—felt like the wind was calling to his wolf and saying *you are home*. Now it just reminded him of how messed up he really was.

Jace pulled open the massive fridge—his mom was used to feeding the hungry shifter hordes that passed through, so it was well-stocked. He snagged some sandwich makings. The ghostly white light blasted through the expansive kitchen, then shut off as the door swung shut. He blinked as his eyes adjusted, and the house creaked again. Only…

Jace froze. He grew up here. He knew the house sounds. *That* was someone on the stairs he just came down. He casually shuffled to the kitchen island and set down the meats and condiments. He held still for a moment, listening. Drawing in a breath. *Scenting.*

Light floral scent. *No one he'd scented before.*

With light bare-footed steps, Jace dashed back through the open kitchen door, skirted the dining table, and rounded the corner to the great room. Halfway up the stairs was a figure in a black hoodie. Jace knew this house like his own face—he didn't need to look to avoid the end tables and floor lamps. He reached the stairs before the intruder could even turn around.

Jace grabbed the hoodie first, yanking it back to get a chokehold, then wrapped his arm around the neck. He pivoted, trying to wrestle the guy down, but his mom must have been polishing the stairs again because his feet went out from under him. They both tumbled the five steps to the landing below. Jace kept his grip, but this must be a kid or something—the hooded figure was lightweight and skinny. No heft to him at all.

Then he shifted in Jace's arms, sliding out of his grip and leaving nothing but clothes behind. Jace shoved aside the hoodie and jeans and scrambled after the wolf, who was making time through the great room. Jace knew there was only one way out—through the back kitchen door. He dashed down the side hall, surged through the kitchen side door, and tackled the wolf before it could make it to the back. Which was great for stopping the intruder from escaping, but now he had to keep hold of a wolf three times stronger than Jace's human form—with razor sharp claws and snapping jaws trying to catch his face. He wrestled it to the floor, holding it from behind. Its claws scrabbled against the low cabinets and pushed them back along the floor. Jace's head banged against the kitchen door in his struggle to keep hold, and the wolf's strength was almost too much for him. His brain caught up to what was happening, and he realized—this wolf was being strangely quiet throughout all this. Was this some kind of prank by one of the stray shifter kids his mom had taken in?

Jace opened his mouth to call for help—he had a house full of shifters who could actually shift and chase this asshole kid down if he got loose—but Jace's words were cut off when the wolf shifted back to human.

*This was no kid.*

A naked girl—no, she was very much a *woman*—was suddenly in his arms, struggling against his hold. He huffed out surprise, but before he could let her loose, she squirmed around so her very ample breasts were now pressed against his bare chest. Then she grabbed the back of his head in both hands... *and kissed him.*

The man in him froze in shock, but his beast nearly burst out of his skin. While Jace struggled to hold back his wolf, his very human mouth responded automatically to the hot demands of her tongue. Her legs wrapped around his waist, and his cock sprang to life, pressing hard against the naked heat of her body. It took him a full two seconds to make sure his wolf was under control—then he regained control over his human body as well, wrenching his mouth away from hers and grabbing hold of her shoulders to shove her away.

With her legs locked around him, she didn't go far.

"What the fuck?" Jace gasped out the words, breathing hard. The woman in his arms was gorgeous—twenty-five-ish, creamy white skin, black hair spilling down to her heaving breasts, which were large and perfectly round with nipples puckered so tight they made his mouth water. She didn't say anything, just stared at him with wide eyes, dark as midnight—her lips were slightly swollen and red from their wild kiss.

If you could even call it a kiss. More like an assault. Who *was* this girl?

She blinked, as if she was stunned too—then she shoved away from him.

"Oh no, you don't!" Jace scrambled after her. He caught her by the ankle before she could get to her feet, then he tugged her off-balance. He cushioned her fall but then twisted to pin her, hands above her head, flat on the cool stone tiling of his mom's kitchen floor. He'd somehow managed to straddle her in the process.

She locked gazes with him for an intense moment, then her eyes raked down his chest and landed on his rock-hard erection, which was tenting out his sleep pajamas

She flicked her gaze back up and gave him a crooked smile. "I guess you're the kind who likes it rough."

What in the actual fuck? "I'm the kind who doesn't like people breaking into his house." His voice was still breathy from the fight.

"*Your* house?" Her voice was amazingly calm for being naked under a stranger. "Are you one of the River brothers, then?"

He squinted at her. "Who the hell are you?"

She glanced up at his hands pinning her wrists to the floor, then smirked at him again. "Are we going to do this interrogation naked? If so, might be more fun if you lose those adorable sleep pants."

His mouth fell open. This girl had more brass than most generals he knew. "If I let you up, are you going to run? Because I have an entire house full of shifters who would be happy to hunt you down."

She sighed and rolled her eyes. "I let you catch me, didn't I?"

"*Let* me—" The wolf in him growled, and he didn't like how she was getting a rise out of more than just his cock, which was embarrassing enough. He released her wrists and shoved off her. As she slowly got up from the floor, he ground out, "You left your clothes by the front door. But if you run for it, I'm not going to be so nice next time."

She threw a flirtatious smile over her shoulder. "Promises, promises."

Her hips swayed as she took her time strolling from the kitchen toward the front. He followed close behind, in case she decided to bolt after all. He was *pissed*—full-on angry at this girl and her attitude and the fact that she had broken into the safehouse with zero obvious remorse or concern—but *damn*, that walk was doing things to his cock.

The moonlight kissed her pale skin as she stepped across the great room, no big hurry, and when she bent over to pick up her clothes—*holy fuck*. He knew she was putting herself on display on purpose, trying to manipulate her way out of this with promises of sex… but the wolf inside him was stirring, and that made Jace's heart pound with fear more than lust.

This girl was *dangerous* to him—in a way human girls never were. Which was precisely why his preferred mode of sexual release was a quick hookup with a human female in a smoke-filled bar in the city. Or more often, his own hand and a hot fantasy about claiming a mate… something that would never happen in reality. But he never tangled with female shifters, even if they were just looking for fun and not actually shopping for a mate. He couldn't take the chance. But he also couldn't look away from the show this shifter girl was putting on—every movement was a sensuous tease. She made slipping on jeans hotter than ripping them off. Which was exactly what his cock was twitching for, in spite of the rock-solid knowledge that it wasn't going to happen.

However, he was definitely going to fantasize about this later.

When she was finally dressed, her smile shone in the moonlight. "You better wipe up the drool, River boy."

He ignored that—it was a show she obviously wanted him to watch, and he needed her to know it wasn't going to work. Plus he needed to cool this whole thing down, including his raging hard-on, and find out exactly what she was doing here.

Jace strode across the great room until he was face to face with her. "Are you going to tell me who you are now? Or do I have to haul out the torture sticks?"

She frowned at his cold look, then matched it with a defiant one of her own. "Are you going to tell me why you didn't shift?"

He mouth dropped open, just for a second, then he snapped it shut and scowled. "Let me be clear about this: you're going to explain why you're breaking into my house, and you're going to do it *right now.*"

She leaned back and threw a pitying look in his direction. "Oh… I see… you *can't.*"

He couldn't help the growl that escaped. "I *can* shift. I choose not to." *Dammit,* how did she get under his skin so fast? He sucked in a breath and tried to regain his calm. "Are you going to answer my question, or do I have to bring in my pack to persuade you?"

She glanced at the front door, but lucky for her, she decided not to make a run for it.

She turned back to study him, folding her arms across her chest and cocking her head to the side. "Why didn't you just shift to catch me?"

"That's really none of your business." He was glad to hear his voice returning to its normal cool. "And you've got three seconds to come clean."

"That offer of naked interrogation is still on the table." She smirked at him again.

"Two."

The smirk faded, and her voice dropped. "Look, I don't need any trouble—"

"One." He glanced up the stairs where the River pack was still slumbering away. One howl would bring them down.

The girl threw up her hands. "Okay, all right."

He waited.

She pursed her lips and hesitated. Then she said, "My name is Piper Wilding."

Jace narrowed his eyes, but he didn't recognize her. Then again, he'd only met a few of the Wilding pack members personally. They were a different breed—still fiercely loyal like a pack should be, but looser in their organization. Whereas Jace and his brothers and their pack all worked for the River brothers' security company, Riverwise, the Wilding's were literally all over the map. Research professors, military, lawyers… they each went their separate way, not just in Seattle, but all over the world. And they had a reputation for being… *unstable*. He'd personally encountered the Wilding brand of crazy—most recently when Terra Wilding tried to crawl into his bed upstairs after Jaxson turned her down. She was an artist who normally lived downtown, but she had been hiding out at the safehouse after they'd rescued her baby sister Cassie.

Terra was a black-haired tornado.

Not unlike the girl standing before him.

"A Wilding," Jace finally said, nodding. "I should have known by the way you wrapped your legs around me before saying hello."

She bit her lip. "You'll never know how great that could have been, River boy."

He hated the effect that had on his cock, which was finally starting to settle down.

"I don't think I'll miss explaining the smell to my mother," he said, keeping his voice ice cold. "And besides, that doesn't really explain anything. We have a doorbell. You could have used it." The Wildings might be hot-blooded, but they really weren't completely insane. Some were even decent and reasonable, like Daniel Wilding, the Army grunt who helped out with their last mission. And who was also parked upstairs, waiting to help them track down Agent Smith and the other captured shifters.

The smoldering sexiness dropped off Piper's face. "I'm not really supposed to be here, River boy."

"No kidding." He glared at her. "And my name is Jace."

"*Jace.*" She rolled his name around in her mouth in a way that had him thinking about tearing her clothes off again. *Damn,* he really had to get that under control. "Well, Jace River, *The Wolf Who Chooses Not To Shift*… I'm not supposed to be *here,* as in Seattle. But I need to see my brother, Daniel. And when I heard you had stashed him and my cousins up here…" She shrugged. "I needed to reach him without alerting the rest of the Wilding family network."

"Have you heard of a cell phone?" He looked askance at her. This story wasn't holding up. "They're a real handy invention. Reduces fatalities from breaking and entering a hundred fold."

She gave him a small smile that didn't completely piss him off… because it was the first one that seemed like it might be real. "Can't fool you, can I, *Jace?*" Then the smile dropped off. "Daniel and I… well, how can I put this?"

"How about the truth?" he asked, coolly.

"We don't talk. Ever. I'm the blackest of sheep in a

pack filled with nothing but black sheep. And Daniel's one of the straighter arrows. And yet… I need his help."

"So a phone call wouldn't cut it." Strangely, he believed her. With so many wild cards in a single pack, no wonder they were scattered to the winds. He couldn't imagine not speaking to his own brothers, but the River pack was different. *Different* meaning *normal,* not insane.

Piper nodded, and her face opened up like she was amazed he understood. This softer expression stirred something inside him—something like sympathy for being the outsider in a pack of crazy wolves—but Jace shut that down fast. If there was one thing he'd already figured out about this one, it was that she was a master at manipulation.

Piper ducked her head and said softly, "Daniel and I have a younger brother, Noah. He's good people." She looked up, eyes round and wide. "The best kind, in fact. And I'm not completely sure, but… I think something's happened to him. He's gone missing, and everything I've done to find him has come up zeroes. You have to believe me—coming here is my last resort."

That had the ring of truth, but Jace still raised his eyebrows. "Missing shifter? Sounds like you're in the right place. Daniel hasn't said anything about a missing brother, though."

She frowned. "Noah was stationed overseas. Army, like Daniel."

Which made sense. Jace nodded. "Sporadic contact. No reason why family stateside would know. At least, not right away." He sucked in a breath. Missing military shifters? Overseas? This thing just got bigger in a way he didn't like. *At all.* "You could have just said that in the first place. If there's an Army brother missing, we're going to find him. Double that for a fellow shifter."

She smiled, and this one was definitely real. It stirred something inside him again, both man and wolf. Maybe she wasn't *all* manipulation. Of course, that only made this hot shifter female even more dangerous to him. But none of that mattered.

A missing brother-in-arms trumped everything.

He tipped his head toward the stairs. "Let's go."

# CHAPTER 2

*God, what a mess.*

All Piper had to do was sneak into a mountain estate and convince her brother to help her. *Sneaking in* was supposed to be the easy part. How many times had she infiltrated buildings, lifted documents, and planted surveillance? *Come on, Piper.* Granted, she wasn't normally tackling a house full of shifters. And she should have anticipated at least one of them being a night wanderer. Not only had she been caught, but she'd been forced to spill a ton of intel to a man she didn't even know.

An extremely hot man, but still. *Sloppy work.*

Piper winced internally as she quietly followed Jace River up the creaky wooden steps of his rambling estate. The man was hotness personified, climbing the stairs in nothing but pajama pants and bare feet. She's already had the pleasure of being pressed up against his sublimely-muscled chest. It had been so long since she'd been that up-close-and-personal with a shifter... she'd forgotten how freaking gorgeous the men could be. And that kiss... *sweet mercy* that was hot. She'd meant to distract him for a moment so she could make her getaway, but then her wolf had insisted they stay and ride that big hunk of shifter for all he was worth.

*That* was unexpected.

Usually, her wolf had only a mild interest in the men that Piper enjoyed. And she'd enjoyed *a lot.* She figured a variety of male bed partners would make up for her vow to never take a mate—that somehow a large quantity of lovers might compensate for the lack of that one, mythical, magical shifter mate who was supposed to rock her world. It hadn't quite worked out that way, so she shouldn't be surprised that her wolf was all hot and heavy for the first shifter she'd kissed in *years.* And when Jace's tall, broad-shouldered body had responded to her epic diversionary kiss—both she and her wolf became *very* aware that he wasn't *small* in any dimension. Piper was certain any woman in his bed would be well satisfied. Her wolf probably thought this meant something. Like she was reconsidering *the vow*—which she definitely was not.

But her wolf wouldn't shut up about it, still panting and stomping her paws and craving this shifter's fangs in her flesh, magically binding them forever. Even now, as Piper climbed the stairs, her wolf was drooling over the man's sculpted V-shaped back, which tapered smoothly down to his pajama pants and ended in a tight rear end that moved like muscular seduction under those thin flannels. Her wolf was dead-sure that bedding this man would be a pleasure like she'd never known.

Okay, Piper could see her wolf's point about that.

It was a good thing she had put on a show of trying to seduce him because her real arousal scent would have given her away. While all the talk of hot sex was just that—*talk*—a part of her couldn't help wishing this Jace River hunk had been a little less… *controlled*.

She kept her sigh of regret for lost chances inside as Jace led her down the hallway, ostensibly to her brother's room. She had to prepare herself for this, now that the distraction of being caught by a ridiculously hot shifter had scrambled her focus.

*Finding Noah.* That was all she needed in life. Make sure her kid brother—the good one, the only Wilding to ever give a damn about her—had not actually wandered off and gotten himself killed somewhere in Afghanistan. Once she knew he was safely running normal missions— as if being deployed was ever safe, but still—then she could go back to her life of traveling to exotic locales to track down the bad guys and bed down the good ones. And ignoring the world of shifters as much as possible. Then her wolf could go back to sleep and stop dreaming of mates she would never have.

Jace tapped lightly at the door to Daniel's room. Piper scented her brother's woodsy-yet-charcoal-undertone natural smell through the rough-carved wood. The Army must have taught him to sleep light because it only took a moment before a shuffle inside the room preceded the door cracking open.

Daniel's hair was bed-tousled, but his eyes were sharp. They landed on Jace first. "Hey, man, what's up?" But the last of his words faded as his gaze found Piper. He rolled his eyes, then briefly squeezed them shut, like the mere sight of her was causing him gastrointestinal pain.

*Nice to see you too, bro.* She bit down on her lips to keep the retort inside. Be cool, get in, get what you need, get out. This had been her mantra all the way up the mountain. She just needed to execute on it now.

Jace seemed on top of the interaction, but he just whispered, "We need to talk."

The house had already slept through her scuffle with Jace downstairs, but it would still be better to get behind closed doors before they started this conversation. In case it got a little heated.

Daniel shook his head but stepped back, gesturing them both into his room. He didn't bother with a light— the moon put a silvery glow on everything enough to see—he just closed the door behind them. The River pack had a pretty nice setup here. High-end rustic furniture. Real paintings on the wall. Thick tapestries as throw rugs. Someone had money, but they used it in understated ways.

Daniel folded his arms and looked to Jace. "What's she done now?"

Jace's eyes narrowed. "Couldn't honestly tell you. But she's got a message I think you might want to hear."

Piper lifted an eyebrow in Jace's direction. *So…* the River brother wasn't going to spill anything about their slap-slap-kiss downstairs. Interesting choice. She snuck a glance at Jace's sleep pants—they were no longer sporting the erection that made her mouth water. He was probably trying to forget the whole thing as quickly as possible.

Daniel turned to her. "Why are you here, Piper?"

She opted to cut straight to it. "Noah is missing."

Daniel's arms unlocked. "What do you mean, missing?"

"Missing, as in *not found*. As in *not where he's supposed to be*. Come on, Daniel, I know you went to college. They must have taught you something there."

He growled at her, and she had to keep her smile in check. And remember her purpose.

"I just skyped with him a couple weeks ago, when I arrived stateside," Daniel said, his tone solidly in the *Piper is freaking for no reason* position. "They probably just shut down the comms at the MWR. He said they had some kind of security breach and might not be able to communicate for a while."

Piper frowned. And Jace was giving her the side-eye like he thought she broke into his house and then *lied* about Noah going missing. But Noah hadn't said anything about the MWR—Morale, Welfare, and

Recreation Center—being closed when they last texted, five days ago.

"I don't contact him through the *Rec Center,* Daniel," she said, trying to match his patronizing tone. "And I'm telling you, he's gone radio silent."

Daniel folded his arms. "Oh, that's right. You're the *spy girl* now."

"Counterintelligence." She glared at him, fully aware of how little he thought of her work, even though it was key to keeping grunts like him and Noah alive. It was like he thought she was CIA or NSA or something. A rival agency, not support. "But hey, thanks for playing and keeping up with the pieces on the board."

He snarled, but she just ignored that... because something gnawed at her about what he said. The skype setups at the MWR were how Noah normally phoned home, but Piper wasn't "home" in Seattle any more than absolutely necessary—and when she was abroad, it was never anywhere she could openly skype with a U.S. Army grunt in some public internet cafe. That was the whole reason she had set up their back-channel comm system in the first place—so she could keep tabs on her kid brother while he was off fighting the bad guys in the worst parts of the world. Their calls had started out weekly, but serving your country generally involved long stretches of extreme boredom punctuated by brief moments of sheer terror. Soon the check-ins were daily, and sometimes they text-chatted for over an hour. And he never missed a check-in unless he was in the middle of a firefight.

If the MWR was actually down… she would have heard about it. If nothing else, Noah would have reported the moaning and complaining of his fellow grunts.

"Wait… you're *counterintelligence?*" Jace asked, bringing her out of her rabbit-hole of thought about that little mystery. He was surprised, but there was more respect in his voice than she ever got from Daniel. Or their father.

She gave Jace a tight smile. "Defense Civilian Intelligence Specialist, working for the Army abroad," she clarified quickly, remembering Jace said he was Army, too. Or she supposed ex-Army now with the River brothers' security business. She did do a *little* research before she decided to break in. "Which means I'm boot dust to some." Piper threw a glare at Daniel, then turned back to Jace, who was keeping a pretty good poker face about the whole thing. "Mostly I just do collective CI— the kind of counterintelligence that collects intel on the bad guy spies. I'm not in offensive operations." Which meant she wasn't out there actively engaging enemy agents to turn them or playing double agent and feeding them false intel. Of course, if she *were,* she certainly wouldn't say so. And there were times when that line got pretty fuzzy.

"I guess that explains why you didn't use the doorbell." Jace's smirk said he was more amused than offended by that now. She supposed that was good. And that flirty smile of his was doing things to her nether parts that she really needed to ignore. *Focus, Piper.*

Daniel snorted—his derision was a lot more familiar. "You just broke in, didn't you? Nice." He shook his head like she was a delinquent teen he didn't know what to do with. "Look, big sister—why don't you just use your fancy spy skills to figure out the big conspiracy about where Noah's been reassigned and let the rest of us sleep?"

"He's not just on an op somewhere!" Piper shot back. "He would have told me." Plus this MWR thing was ramping up her nerves. Why would Noah say that... unless he expected to go dark for some reason? And why not tell *her?* Warn her, at least. So she didn't panic. Like she was. *Right now.*

Daniel gave her his best impression of their father—

all authority and derision toward the little girl who was such a disappointment to him. "Maybe he found something better to do than chat with his sister. Or they confiscated his phone. Or maybe, just maybe, he dropped that extremely expensive satellite phone you gave him in the latrine."

His smirk and his words were just making her stomach wind tighter and tighter. All that was possible… but she didn't believe any of it.

"Right," she huffed. "Has to be a phone down the crapper. Because nothing else ever goes sideways in Afghanistan." Her glare darkened, and if she didn't know Daniel could easily take her in a fight, she was tempted to shift and give him a face full of claws for not showing more concern about his little brother. Because something could be very wrong, and as far as she could tell, he cared more about giving her crap than he did about Noah's safety. Daniel was more a junior version of their dad each time she saw him. It had been a year since the last time— obviously nowhere near long enough.

Daniel just held her glare, not backing down.

"You know what?" Piper hissed. "You're right. This was obviously a mistake." She turned on her heel and got halfway to the door before a hand stopped her with a gentle tug on her elbow. Daniel knew better than to touch her, so she reeled in her instinct to whirl with a handful of claws out.

It was Jace. "Hang on," he said, glancing back at Daniel. "If Noah's missing, I meant what I said about finding him. We went after Cassie and brought her back. We'll do the same for him."

Piper pulled her elbow out of his grasp, but gently. "I know. I'm not entirely out of the Wildling pack loop. I heard about what you guys did for Cassie." She glared at Daniel. "There are a few Wildings who still think I'm worth talking to."

Daniel rolled his eyes. "Oh, for the love of God!" He pointed a finger at her. *"You* were the one who decided to leave—"

"As if you even noticed—"

"How could I not *notice?* You stormed out like a class five Hurricane!"

*"You* don't have to deal with the almighty Colonel—"

*"I* deal with him all the time. Somehow, it's never a problem."

"No, it wouldn't be, *for you,* now would it?"

"Whatever!" He threw out his hands. "It's never *you,* is it, Piper? You've always done exactly what you—"

*"Enough!"* Jace's voice cut through their squabbling like an alpha command—Piper winced, but she noted with satisfaction that Daniel did, too. And that *tone*… it sent a thrill through her wolf that had her lady parts a-flutter again. Piper shoved that aside. This wasn't an alpha thing, she told herself. It was an *age* thing—Jace was twenty-eight, according to his bio, and Piper was only twenty-five, Daniel a mere twenty-three. Noah was just a baby at twenty-one, which was why she had looked out for him her whole life—because no one else did, and he was just a kid when their mom died.

No one deserves to grow up completely without a mom—one of the many reasons she'd decided never to take a mate.

Jace was staring them down, each in turn, and Piper's insides were warring as to whether they liked that commanding look or hated it. Probably both. And she hated that she liked it, so that was mixed in there, too. *Gah!* She was a freaking mess with this. Piper backhanded her wolf's hungry pant for more of Jace's commanding touch, in words and flesh. Her wolf went off to sulk in the corner.

Jace let out a low, long breath of patience. "I do not give a *fuck* what your family problems are," he finally ground out. "But I care very much about whether I've got Army shifters going missing. Or not. Both of you need to knock this shit off and work together to figure this out. Then you can go back to whatever passes for family relations in the Wilding pack. But not before we get solid intel on whether your brother is missing."

Daniel's eyes narrowed. "You don't know my sister like I do, Jace. She lies for a living now, but she's always been a manipulator. You can't trust her."

Piper cringed—partly because it was true, but mostly because she was afraid it would turn Jace against her just as he was starting to come around. He turned back to her, doubt creating shadows on his face.

"Soldiers get reassigned all the time," Jace said, carefully. "Maybe he's just gone dark for a mission. What makes you think he's gone missing?"

"Because I talk to him *every day*." She lifted her chin to Daniel. "We have an actual relationship, unlike this hot mess." Back to Jace, with a lowered voice. "He wouldn't just go dark with no warning. I swear. Something is wrong." That much was the God's honest truth. She prayed he would hear it in her voice.

Jace frowned and nodded. "All right." He took a breath. "In the morning, we'll discuss this with my brothers and make a game plan—"

*"Morning?"* Piper's voice hiked up. "Why do you think I'm here in the middle of the night? We need to get on this, like yesterday!" She tried to bring her voice back down to reasonable. "Daniel has access to the Joint Base. He's got clearance. I can't even get on site, but *he* could get in there anytime and access their records, see what's happened—"

Daniel's mouth fell open. "You want me to hack the Joint Base records?" He acted as if she'd asked him to streak naked across the base. Actually, no—he would have laughed at that. This was worse. Much worse. This was their father's territory, and she was asking him to piss all over it.

"Daniel's right," Jace said, his voice calm. "You can't go blustering into—"

*"Blustering?"* She completely failed to keep her voice down. "I could do it with my hands tied behind my back. Even *this* blundering amateur—"

Daniel growled at her. "I'm not risking my security clearance for this!"

"It's a bad idea, Piper," Jace said, but his voice was strained again. "We know from when Cassie was taken that they are government types involved in this, but we don't know how far it goes. Let me and my brothers handle this from the outside, so we don't tip them off."

*Dammit.* He wasn't going to help her after all. "Sure. Let's take our time. Meanwhile, Noah's in a dark cell somewhere being tortured." She could hardly keep the tremble out of her voice.

"We don't know that!" Daniel protested.

"You're right," she spat back. "He could already be dead." She was seriously going to give him some facial scars as a souvenir before she left.

"Okay, okay!" Jace threw his hands up, holding Piper and Daniel apart. "Let's cool this down a bit, shall we?" He pointed to Daniel. *"You* sit tight and think about what we can do for intel. And stop being an ass." Then he turned to Piper. *"You* get a guest room and park it for a while. And stop assuming the worst before we know anything at all, okay?"

Her breath was heaving, and she wanted to tell him to fuck off—it wasn't *his* brother that was possibly being tortured to death. Instead, she did a quick scan of the room. Daniel had always been a neat freak, and the Army had just reinforced those habits. Everything was neatly put away, including a light-weight jacket hanging on the back of the bedroom door.

She looked back to Jace's questioning expression and wrestled her voice into a semblance of conciliation. "All right. We'll talk about this in the morning." She turned her back on him and strode to the door, counting on him to take a moment to talk to Daniel before they left.

"We're going to work this out," Jace said to her brother.

She took that instant to slip her hand inside her brother's jacket and get the one thing she really needed. Then she pulled open the door and marched into the hallway, covering the sway of the jacket with the motion of the flung-open door. She slipped her prize into her front pocket as she went.

Jace's footsteps followed quickly after her. "Hey," he said, catching her by the elbow again. "This way." He nodded down the hall in the opposite direction.

She swung around and followed him down a couple turns in this gigantic estate of his to a room similar to Daniel's but smaller. Jace opened the door and gestured her inside.

"It's going to be all right, Piper." His voice was gentle, and the fire in his eyes had softened. "Hopefully, Noah's completely fine, just holed up somewhere. And if not, we're going to find him."

"Sure." She tried to sound positive, but her skills were failing her—too much personal entanglement was eroding her ability to do her job. Once she found Noah, she was going to take that assignment in Bolivia she'd been avoiding and get lost in hot Latin men for a while. Get back to her normal state of not giving a shit about anything except work. And her baby brother.

Jace frowned. His eyes were deep brown, like Noah's, and filled with a genuine concern that made her face heat. Like he saw right through her, which somehow both thrilled and terrified her. Plus the scruff on his face, at least a day's worth, and the bed-tossed hair standing on end just made him insanely sexy in the moonlight. Her wolf wanted nothing more than to drag him into the room with her and spend the next couple hours finding out just how delicious Jace River's body could be. But she had a mission—a brother to find, alive or dead—and taking Jace River to bed wasn't going to help with that. At least… not anymore.

"We *are* going to find him," Jace repeated, softly, reassuring. "I'll come get you when everyone's up."

"Okay." She schooled her face to hide the roiling emotion under her skin.

He nodded and turned to leave.

She almost called him back to thank him—for caring, for putting Daniel in his place, for trying to reassure her—but she held herself in check. Wouldn't matter anyway.

She didn't plan on seeing him again.

# CHAPTER 3

J ace finished the last bite of his sandwich just as the sun came up.

The warm glow spilled through the windows of the great room and painted the kitchen's stainless steel appliances rosy red. The house was just now starting to stir—which was remarkable, given that Piper, Daniel, and he had practically brawled over rescuing her brother Noah—but the sounds of people awakening upstairs meant his time was running out.

He'd been using his tablet to search for possible

disappearances of military grunts like Noah, but the information he could access publicly from the safehouse was extremely limited. His office at Riverwise was better equipped—there he had access to a couple private military networks where he could scan the back-channel chatter. Nothing that was security-related, but if there were suddenly a lack of communication from a lot of personnel, that would show up. Once his brothers, Jaxson and Jared, rolled out of their respective beds, the three of them could form a plan on how to tackle this. Maybe a trip to the office for more extensive research. Or maybe Daniel could get them into the Joint Base. They might have better access there if they could get away with it. The trick would be poking around without tipping their hand to Agent Smith—or whatever his real name was.

Just as Jace was stowing his now-clean sandwich plate and trying to decide whether to barge in on Jaxson and Olivia's post-mating honeymoon, the pair stumbled into the kitchen, bleary-eyed and smelling of the hot sex they no doubt had been having all night long.

"Hey, you two," Jace said with a growl. "Can you wipe off the smiles? The rest of us are trying to have a miserable morning." He couldn't help the twinge inside when he thought about Jaxson finally finding his true mate. Olivia was wonderful, and Jace didn't begrudge his brother a second of their happiness, but it was hard to look them in the face and know they had something he never would.

At least now their pack had a fully mated alpha to lead them and lend them strength. Jace could have filled that role, except for the glaring fact that he couldn't shift— not without endangering the very people he was supposed to protect—and due to that, he could never mate. Other than that, he was the perfect candidate! The truth was, Jaxson was the right brother to be their pack alpha, but Jace hadn't, technically, even submitted to him—at least, not since Jace was discharged. He had pledged his allegiance in human form, but that meant no magic bond to strengthen his alpha and his pack as a whole. If he had been able to take a mate, that bond would have been even stronger.

Just one more way Jace was unable to fulfill his duties.

He shoved those thoughts deep into the dark place where his inner wolf stayed locked away, at least during the daylight hours. He needed to stay on task, and right now, that meant helping Piper find her missing brother, Noah.

"Good morning, brother!" Jaxson declared with excessive joy, his hand tucked at Olivia's waist and a smile wide on his face.

She gestured to the window behind her, with its view of the blue-tinged mountains, now turning hazy with the pink dawn and early morning mist. "How can you be miserable on a gorgeous day like this?" she asked.

"Some of us didn't enjoy the night quite as much as others," Jace said with a smirk.

Olivia blushed, but her smile and glowing happiness stayed strong.

Jaxson's grin dimmed when he finally took a good look at Jace. He hadn't bothered with a mirror this morning, or a shave, but he was sure there were black shadows under his eyes and the makings of a ragged beard. And Jaxson was always worrying about him even on the best of days.

His brother tried to resurrect his smile as he lifted his chin to Jace. "Seriously, man. Jared is the brother who's supposed to be miserable all the time, not you."

"Yeah, well, I need to talk to him, too." Jace glanced toward the stairs. No one had yet wandered down, and Jared slept hard. "I'll pay you hundred dollars to wake him. Last time, he nearly took my face off with those daggers he claims are claws."

"Something's up," Jaxson said, frowning. It was a statement. Neither of them would bother waking Jared unless it was an emergency.

"We had a visitor last night," Jace said, "and she's still here. Daniel's sister, Piper, crashed the safehouse at three in the morning. Says her brother is missing. A younger one, not Daniel."

"Missing?" Jaxson's scowl grew darker. "And you think it's connected to the others?"

Jace shrugged. They had so little intel to go on. "I think we need to get busy and find this Agent Smith character. I hate to interrupt your honeymoon, but…"

Jaxson pulled Olivia closer to him, fingers laced together. "We'll have a real honeymoon once this is all over, right, baby?"

She nodded, a tight smile on her face. "Missing shifters trumps everything." She looked at Jace. "Do we know when Piper's brother went missing?"

Jace rubbed the back of his neck. "Not exactly. Not even completely sure he *is* missing. His name's Noah. And he's an Army grunt."

"*Military* shifters?" Jaxson loosened his hold on Olivia and straightened.

"Yeah, and he went missing overseas. I don't like it, Jaxson. Could be more kinds of bad than I even want to think about. And Piper is crazy freaked out. Of course, she's a Wilding, so…" He left that hanging because the Wilding's really took after their pack name.

"I've never met her," Jaxson said, frowning. "Is she another Terra?"

Jace huffed a short laugh. "Yeah, if Terra were counterintelligence with a penchant for breaking and entering." He shook his head. The whole pack was clearly *out there,* but you didn't get into counterintelligence, even as a civilian, without having something on the ball.

Jaxson's eyebrows lifted. "Counterintelligence? Alrighty, then."

"Yeah." Jaxson had to fight to rein in the smirk. "She's a handful." He'd actually *had* a handful of her, and his wolf wasn't forgetting that any time soon. She was unpredictable, and she pissed him off with her recklessness, but *damn,* she had felt good when he had his paws on her. There were all kinds of smoldering hotness inside that short, voluptuous frame of hers, and he halfway hoped that, if they found Noah, she might be grateful the way Terra had been when they rescued her little sister Cassie. The *crawling in his bed* kind of grateful.

Terra wasn't his type, but Piper… Jace's wolf surged up from the dark pit, making Jace suck in a breath. Then again, maybe not. His wolf wanted her in his bed even more than Jace. And that was flat dangerous.

Just one more thing his wolf would ruin for him.

Jace blew out the breath he'd been holding. "The thing is, I'm not entirely sure her brother's actually missing. Have we started work on tracking down Agent Smith? I know you've been… *busy*… but I thought Jared was working intel on this last night. Do you know?"

"I'll go boot him out of bed and get him down here. See what he's got." Jaxson trotted over to the stairs and headed up.

Olivia bit her lip and looked as anxious as Jace felt. He genuinely regretted intruding upon their happiness, but getting through this would require all of their pack working together—and probably pulling in help from the Wildings as well. Noah was part of their pack, after all. But all the local area packs looked to the River pack wolves for leadership on this kind of thing, given Riverwise was private security and almost all their pack had military backgrounds.

Olivia edged closer to him, anxiety deepening her frown. "I know you don't trust witches, but I promise you, Jace, I love your brother like I've never loved any man on earth. Or shifter."

Jace held up a hand and waved away her concern—she was half witch, and he generally despised the species, but he knew she was different. And she had saved Jaxson from his own dark secret, one Jace hadn't even seen. "It's obvious you make Jaxson happy. Not much I can object to with that. And the mating bond between the two of you makes the pack stronger. It's all good, just took me by surprise is all. Besides, having a few allies in a certain powerful downtown Seattle coven might help us unravel this thing." It hadn't occurred to him before, but maybe Olivia's family—the Damon coven—would be able to help them track down Noah. Or at least see if he truly was missing.

"Not sure the coven really wants to be involved in pack business." Olivia grimaced. "But I'll do anything I can to help."

Jace gave her a sharp nod. He'd take help from the witches, if offered, but he certainly wasn't going to go begging… and he really only trusted Olivia to have shifters' best interests at heart.

Pounding footsteps down the stairs made him think Jaxson had managed to rouse Jared from his typical crashed-out state. The oldest River brother had his own nightmarish past, but he was better at working it out than Jace. And Jared wasn't a danger to anyone. He could shift and let his wolf form run out all of his horror at the things that had happened and the things he had done. Jace didn't have that luxury, not when there were people around who could be hurt by it. Which meant Jared paid his penance by hitting the mountains or the shooting range for endless hours, exhausting himself, and when he hit the sack, he hit it hard. Crashing like the dead man Jace suspected his brother longed to be.

Both his brothers lumbered into the kitchen with Daniel close behind.

"I figured if everyone was getting up…" Daniel shrugged.

Jace just nodded. Piper's brother should be part of this conversation, anyway. Piper too, but Jace wasn't quite ready to deal with her brand of Wilding insanity just yet. Better to have a plan first.

Jaxson hooked a thumb toward Jared. "Tell Jace what you were telling me."

Their oldest brother was the largest among them, although none of the River brothers was exactly small. The shifter gene, plus their military training and staying in shape for their business, meant they were all pretty well bulked up. Jaxson was an ex-SEAL and Jace was a former Army medic, but Jared was all Marine. And it showed.

He ran a hand through his hair, which was mussed. His sleep must have been restless at some point, even if he slept like the dead. "I've been trying to access some of the local military information systems. Nothing classified, just poking around to see if anyone has heard of this Agent Smith. And I've uploaded a sketch to our office facial recognition software—it's scanning some of the law enforcement and city-wide camera databases to see if we can track down who this guy really is. It's only been a day since we kicked his ass, but he could have flown that little two-seater airplane anywhere. I kind of doubt we'll get lucky and find him in Seattle."

Daniel spoke up. "If he's got another base of operations nearby, he might stick around."

It was a decent possibility.

"Somehow, I doubt he's gone far," Jace said. "But wherever he is, he's got to be deep undercover. Even if he's not showing his face *now,* he's got to have some history. Maybe cruising up to an ATM to pull out cash for that cheap government suit he was wearing."

Jared snorted. "Yeah, maybe. I'm tapped into all the

databases back at Riverwise. Hasn't pinged anything yet. I've got an alert set up on my phone."

Jace gave him a nod, impressed. Jared was actually bringing his A-game to this, rather than heading off to the forest, per usual, to get lost in the woods—literally and figuratively.

Jaxson gestured to Daniel. "You're Army, right? Where are you stationed while you're stateside?"

Jace grimaced. They'd already had this fight, last night, with Piper.

Daniel's face pinched in, but he kept it cool. "The Joint Base at Lewis-McChord. My father is a Lieutenant Colonel there." He threw a pained look to Jace. "But Piper is right—he's really not the best one to go to for help. Not unless you've already got solid intel."

Jaxson and Jared looked at him, expectantly. "Which we do *not*," Jace reminded them. He turned to Daniel. "I think we need to bring Piper into this. She might have more intel to share than she was willing to give up last night under, er, less than desirable circumstances. Why don't you go fetch her? She's in the last bedroom on the left, end of the hall, upstairs."

Daniel looked like Jace had just asked him to dip his fingers into the latrine. But he turned and jogged off toward the stairs.

Jace waited until he was out of earshot. "Daniel and Piper... *have issues,*" he explained to Jace, Jared, and Olivia. "Last night they had a hell of a fight. Some kind of thing with the dad, the Colonel at the Joint Base. Piper wanted Daniel to use his clearance to get into their systems and poke around, looking for Noah. Daniel was having none of that. But it might not be a bad idea."

"I don't know," Jared said, a skeptical look on his face. "We don't know how far this thing reaches."

"True." Jace crossed his arms tight over his chest. "Maybe Daniel can look around but keep it quiet. Meanwhile, we'll do our research on the outside. If Noah's truly disappeared, it *has* to be connected to this Agent Smith. If we can get a clue as to where he's hiding, that has to help. And if Daniel's careful, he won't violate any classified material protocols and shouldn't raise too many alarm bells." Jace glanced at Olivia. "And maybe we can get a little magical help from our favorite witchy office assistant."

Olivia grinned. "Aunt Gwen's dying to help me learn some spells. I think a seeking spell might be first on the list."

Jared seemed dubious about that, too, but Jaxson had

a small smirk on his face.

"Either way," Jace said, "we need to get on this. If we work together, cover multiple fronts at once, we should make the fastest progress. We already know Agent Smith was experimenting on the prisoners he had before. If he's taking military shifters now—" The sound of bare feet pounding down the stairs cut him off.

Daniel came flying back into the kitchen. "Piper is gone." He rushed the words all out at once.

*Fuck.* Jace hung his head down, shaking it slightly. "Man, I should've known. No way was she settled last night. *Dammit."* Just like a Wilding to run off half-cocked, doing God-knew-what. Probably the craziest thing possible. From what little he knew of Piper, it was probably the most *dangerous* thing possible. Somehow that roused his wolf up from the depths almost as much as her curvy little behind in the moonlight. He growled back at his wolf, shoving him down again, then whipped his head up to look at Daniel. "I don't suppose you have any idea where she's run off to?"

His scowled, the muscles in his jaw working overtime. "I know exactly where she's gone."

# CHAPTER 4

Getting onto the Joint Base wouldn't be that difficult, now that Piper had swiped her brother's identification and base pass. She'd used his ID to create a slightly-modified duplicate, putting some of her counterintelligence skills to good use, but the security just wasn't that tight at the Joint Base to begin with. At least, not at the front gate, where she sat in a line of cars idling in the early morning wait to get waved through.

The sun was just starting to rise over the mountains in

the east. The small guard shack sat under a long corrugated metal roof stretching over the three lanes that marked the entrance. She'd retrieved her car—the one she used when she was in Seattle—to drive to the base rather than take a cab, like she's used to return from the River brothers' safehouse in the mountains, a good hour away. She imagined Jace was looking for her about now, and she couldn't help wondering what his reaction would be when he discovered she took off. Royally pissed, probably. Her wolf had been whining ever since she left, but she doubted Jace's first reaction would be regret that they hadn't ravished each other before she disappeared. Piper rolled her eyes at her wolf's pathetic whimper about that.

The Joint Base was south of Tacoma, a sprawling enterprise of on-base housing, training grounds, workout facilities, and all manner of Army and Air Force operations. The building she was most interested in was near the center of the several mile wide complex—the command center. She hoped Daniel's key card would gain her access to the red-bricked and stoic-looking building… as well as a secure terminal to search for clues as to Noah's location.

Of course, hacking into the Army's database was

highly illegal, but she was doing it for a good cause—and it was something the Army itself should be doing for her brother, if they cared at all about their shifter soldiers. He was just another grunt to them, but he was everything to her. And she worried that his shifter abilities had maybe caught *too much* interest from them. As she well knew, the Army put their soldiers to maximum use, deploying all their assets. Her secret hope was that they'd simply recruited him into some dark program where he was using his shifter abilities to fight the bad guys. She'd even be proud of that.

But she knew her little brother—he would have bragged about that to her. Endlessly.

Piper edged forward in the car line, sandwiched between two rows of pointed orange cones half the size of her vehicle. The guards quickly waved through the people ahead of her, but when she reached the front, the middle-aged one in charge asked for her ID with a short wave of his fingers. She gave it over with a bright smile that she hoped would convince him she had the IQ of a fluffy bunny and posed just as much of a security risk… and couldn't possibly be civilian counterintelligence trying to hack their secure databases. This wasn't her first time convincing people she was something she wasn't, but she couldn't go too far with the dumb girl act. The Joint Base got a lot of civilian traffic, spouses and significant others of soldiers traveling on and off base, but her ID said she had top-level security and thus access to the more secure buildings on the grounds.

The guard took too long to scrutinize her ID. "State your name," he said without looking up. His gruff voice sounded like he'd already been up half the night.

"Daniela Wuldinger. On reassignment from the Senator's office. Temporary."

The guard lifted one eyebrow, still examining her ID. For *far* too long.

A nervous sweat broke out between her shoulder blades, but she kept the smile at full force.

Then he gave her a short nod. "Just a moment, please."

His hard-soled shoes scuffed the pavement of the street, then the concrete of the guard shack floor as he stepped inside to consult with his computer and a fellow guardsman. They were both wearing the desert camouflage that was standard for active-duty personnel on base, as well as a bright yellow reflective vest, presumably for the traffic.

Piper waited, forcing the smile to remain on her

face… as if she had no concerns whatsoever that her completely falsified identification would be discovered. She truly *was* connected to the Senator's office, as a consultant to the defense subcommittee—but her altered ID was a hodge-podge of hers and Daniel's real clearances mixed with a falsified name. She'd conjured worse IDs in much more hostile territories in her operations around the world, but security in the US was actually competent most of the time. Which made it a higher bar she had to hurdle. And this false ID was a slap-dash effort at 4 am in her apartment, not going through her normal chain of command… not least because it would never have been approved.

There was far too much discussion going on in the shack.

When the original guard finally returned to her car, he said, "Welcome to Lewis-McChord, Ms. Wuldinger." He handed her ID back to her.

She did an impressive job of not letting the sigh of relief show.

He leaned in with one hand on top of her car, gave her an appreciative look, and smirked. "You might want to stop by the Soldiers Field House during your stay, Ms. Wuldinger. We're having a Combatives Tournament today. I'm afraid civilians can't compete, but Senator Krepky might want a personal report on the fine fighting form of our active-duty personnel."

She returned his flirtatious grin. "A bunch of sweaty grunts, muscled up and testing their hand-to-hand combat skills? Wouldn't miss *that* for the world. Thank you, Corporal." She mock-saluted him.

He just stepped back, grinned, and waved her through.

Piper had only been on base at Lewis-McChord once before, but the directions around the sprawling military city were fairly straightforward, and she'd mapped out her route anyway. She sailed right past the red-bricked, colonial-style Headquarters with the large brass cannon on the front lawn and headed for the command center, which had the high-security access she needed. It was just a short drive along the nearly-empty early-morning streets, near the center of the base.

Unlike the traditional architecture of Headquarters, the command center was a modern architectural beauty. The designers had mixed traditional red brick with native white granite and thousands of square feet of glass. The 66th Theater Aviation Command (TAC) Readiness Center was the largest and newest command center for the Washington Army National Guard, according to their website. Piper had seen the pictures before, but the building itself was undeniably gorgeous—three stories of soaring glass and steel that let in tons of natural light. She had no doubt her father strutted through the doors like a peacock every morning. But the building was large enough—and she was early enough—that the chances of crossing paths with him should be infinitesimally small.

She hoped.

Two guards with semiautomatic M-16 rifles stood at the entrance, but they were primarily an honor guard, and their brusque looks didn't concern her. Either her ID would pass, or it wouldn't. She swiped it past the detector, the light came up green, and she cruised inside. The two-story entrance had more of the white stone flooring, which was tinged a pale rose by the early-morning sun.

She strode confidently past the reception desk toward the offices on the main floor.

Piper had a lot of experience acting like she knew exactly what she was doing even when she had absolutely no clue. Pretending she was precisely where she belonged was an art. With the right amount of confidence and charm, she'd proven time and again that she could convince almost anyone of anything. It was a kind of game, this mask she put on for the world, not so much a deception—at least for the good guys. The bad guys, she was happy to screw all day long. Not in the literal sense. The only men she allowed in her bed were the ones who had some decency. It was often a fine line, especially in the field, but she had a well-tuned antenna. Knowing the difference between the good guys and the bad could mean walking away or ending up in pieces. That wasn't an exaggeration, even for a rapid-healing shifter like her. And the genuinely good guys were rare, so when she found one, her antenna pinged hard.

*Like with Jace River.* She pushed that unwelcome thought aside. She'd blown her chance with him by bailing and coming here… and she didn't plan to stick around Seattle long enough to have another.

As she wound through the cubicle-land of the command center analysts, Piper held her head high, met the curious stares with a smile, and occasionally gave someone a friendly wave. Anyone at their desk at 6 AM was either working the early morning shift or had been there all night. As civilian counterintelligence for the Army, her time in Washington was usually spent in Olympia at the capitol building, consulting with Senator

Krepky's staff for the Senate defense subcommittee. Her clearance, her experience, and the fact that she was a shifter, all made her a resource the Army liked to exploit to keep the political types on their side.

It was a great job, actually, and one she had no desire to lose. Not to mention that her travels conveniently kept her far from this precise building where her father, Lt. Colonel Astor Wilding held court. Ever since she had turned eighteen and stormed out of the house, staying out of her father's orbit had been priority number one. This little mission was trespassing on her father's territory, something she had long ago vowed never to do. But Noah deserved better than to disappear into a black hole and have no one even try to find him.

Once she had made a circuit through the first floor, she subtly tried the access to a stairwell with her key card. *Locked.* She didn't want to trigger any alarms with a repeat attempt, so she made her way to the coffee room and poured herself a brimming, steaming cup. With any luck, the command center would be high enough on the food chain to have decent coffee. Which she certainly needed after being up most of the night. She took a few sips— not bad—then casually strolled back down the hall and ducked into an empty cubicle.

The analyst who owned this ten-by-ten space had either not come in yet or stepped away. In case they'd only made a quick trip to the bathroom, Piper hung out, sipping her coffee and looking like she was just on break. After about three minutes, she set down her cup, eased into the chair, and tapped awake the computer screen.

Her background didn't include a specialization in computer hacking, but she was familiar with military security protocols, and she hopefully had the right ID. It wasn't so much a matter of hacking, as just having the right access to begin with. The computer was locked down, as per protocol, but anyone with standard level access should be able to open it up again. Which she managed with a simple swipe of her key card. The prompt for the central database would be the trick. She'd already constructed a new user and password for her ID—she tapped those in, said a silent prayer, and pressed the enter key.

*Access denied.*

She typed it again hoping she had simply mistyped the first time.

*Access denied.*

*Shit.* Third time was either the charm… or the thing that would set off all the alarm bells. She stood up, ready to make a run for her car, as she carefully typed the string of letters and numbers one more time.

She didn't even finish typing before a shuffle of boots and a click sound made her look up. Standing at the entrance to her cubicle was a burly man in camouflage with an M-16 pointed at her head.

Her hands whipped up into the air. "Hey, no need to get excited! I just was checking my email."

He didn't move. Half a breath and a flurry of stomping boots later, four more rifles appeared over the top of the short cubicle walls, all pointed at her head.

"Hey, now, come on," she said quickly, forcing a smile on her face. "I'm not doing anything."

"Down on your knees," the first one said in a low command that brooked no dissent.

She dissented anyway. "But, I swear, I didn't—"

"Not going to ask you again, Ma'am."

The military politeness sent a shiver through her. The boy was serious. He was prepared to shoot her dead right here in the cubicle.

"Yeah, okay, sure. Just don't… don't shoot, okay?" Piper kept her voice light and scared, like an innocent person would have, even though she was far from that. She slowly sank to her knees, hands behind her head.

The soldiers rushed in and shoved her to the ground.

Somehow, she'd really fucked this up.

# CHAPTER 5

D aniel was convinced Piper would come straight to
the Joint Base, and Jace could understand why: she
had stolen his ID. Which was why they were sitting in the
security office of Lewis-McChord, getting Daniel's
fingerprints and retina scans recorded and cleared
through the system. They'd been there for over an hour,
and the sun was halfway up the sky. Finally, after a hell of
a lot of paperwork even for the military, Daniel scored a
new ID, and they were released. Jace had a restricted-
access visitor's pass, but Daniel had his full security

clearance key card enabled.

Jace glanced at his phone: nearly ten o'clock.

As the two of them strode out of the brick-and-concrete security office near the front gate, Jace asked, "Your dad's a Colonel here, right?" He hadn't wanted to mention it earlier, while they were inside, especially given how it seemed a sensitive issue between Daniel and Piper. But it was pretty relevant to their objectives, given the Colonel surely could have vouched for his son and expedited getting a new ID.

"Yeah." Daniel's face pinched in. "Trust me, the Colonel's not the kind to easily forgive something like losing your ID. It was easier and less painful this way. Plus, I didn't want to explain that Piper was the one who stole it."

Jace looked askance at him. "But if Piper came here directly, wouldn't he already know? Especially if she used your ID to get in? I mean, would that even work? You two look alike, but trust me, no one's going to think she's male."

Daniel grimaced. "She probably altered the ID. And she's probably sneaking around the base without setting off any alarms. It's the kind of thing she's good at." He scowled like there was a history behind that statement.

"Believe me, she doesn't want my father to know she's here. I'm sure she's using all her shiny new spy skills to avoid that."

"So, then, what's our next move?" Jace wasn't familiar with the base. During his time in the Army as a medic he was stationed at Fort Drum in New York, the First Brigade Combat Team, 10th Mountain Division. The 1st BCT deployed to Afghanistan, like Noah Wilding's troop, but Jace discharged over a year ago now, and there had been thousands of soldiers rotating through Afghanistan since then. Still... some of his contacts in the Division might know if soldiers had started to go missing. Jace had already put some feelers out before they left the safehouse.

Daniel gestured to his car. "Next, we go to my office and try to figure out where Piper might be." They hopped in and drove to a large brick-and-white stone building near the center of the base that looked brand-spanking new. Its towering glass and steel architecture was straight out of a design catalog. The sign out front identified it as the Theater Aviation Command (TAC) Readiness Center.

"Your buildings are like flipping cathedrals here," Jace said, with a smirk as they climbed out of the car. "Knew I should've tried to get stationed in Washington."

"It's not all sunshine and sparkly granite," Daniel said, with a grimace. "Working in the same building as your father has drawbacks."

"So, what's the deal with Piper and the Colonel?" Jace didn't want to pry, and he really shouldn't care… but he did. Piper was definitely a full-blooded Wilding—wild and sexy and feisty. Not entirely bad qualities, except for that *wild* part, but the way she'd blown up like a hair-trigger IED when the topic of her father came up made Jace more than a little curious. Yet it was the sad look in her eyes that really drew him in. She'd locked down emotionally there at the end as if she was dead certain she couldn't depend on anyone but herself.

Just Piper against the world.

That gnawed at him. And it kept drawing his wolf uncomfortably close to the surface. No one, but especially a shifter, should ever be that alone in the world. That's what *family* and *pack* were all about.

Jace's father had died a long time ago from an early heart attack, but family was everything in the River pack. And not just blood relatives—the River pack wolves were like brothers. And his mother was a momma wolf to every stray shifter that came through the area. She'd practically adopted several who had taken up residence at the safehouse—they helped keep it running in return for having a family and a home to call their own. As for Jace's actual brothers… Jared and Jaxson were like his own flesh. He couldn't imagine not trusting them, the way Piper obviously didn't trust Daniel or even her own father.

Jace's question still hung in the air, unanswered, as they walked toward the two-story entrance to the Joint Base's command center. He waited until they were past the two heavily-armed honor guards and just inside the glass door.

"Hey, man, I don't want to pry into your family," Jace said, quietly. "It's really none of my business. I just think it's somewhat relevant to our mission here."

"You're right." Daniel tossed a cold look his way. "It's none of your business."

*Okay, then.* Jace arched an eyebrow. *"Do not trespass* sign duly noted."

Daniel growled, but it seemed more in frustration than anger. He stopped before they got much further into the two-story reception area. "Look, I don't mean to be an ass. There's just a lot of private family stuff that went down a long time ago. All you need to know is that

Piper's erratic. My sister's been making shit up since she was a kid. She ran away from home more times than I can count. And she's always done *exactly* whatever she wants to, no matter how difficult that makes life for the rest of us. If she's here on base, we need to find her before my father does. Before she digs herself a hole deeper than I can get her out of."

Daniel's worried look was the first hint Jace had seen of the kind of brotherly concern he expected. So... maybe it *was* in there, just buried under a mountain of bad history.

"Understood." Jace wanted to know more, but they needed to keep their eyes on the prize—making sure Piper wasn't getting sucked into a mess she couldn't handle and finding the truth about Noah's disappearance.

Daniel led the way up to the second floor and a small office with the door that he quickly closed behind him. He logged into his computer and scanned his messages.

"Give me a minute," he said, "and I'll see if there's any hint of on-base unusual activity. Then I'll see what I can do about finding out what happened to Noah."

While Daniel worked his computer, Jace stared out the window at the sprawling campus. Where would Piper have gone? She had to already be on base. Which meant she must've used Daniel's ID. The question was... why hadn't the guards at the gate mentioned anything about that? It should have come up during their security check, at the least. Piper was counterintelligence—did she just waltz in with false ID? Probably. If what Daniel said was correct—and there was no doubt Piper was unpredictable—then maybe she didn't do the logical thing. Maybe she was holding off, laying low until she came up with a better way to access the Joint Base's resources. Then again, the girl who grabbed him and kissed him in his own kitchen, after breaking into his house, didn't seem like the type to hesitate to action.

A knock on the door interrupted his thoughts.

A short brown-haired woman popped her head in the door. "Sir? Your father would like to see you in his office." She ducked her head and closed the door behind her, as if she knew she was delivering bad news and needed to escape quickly.

Jace threw a fast look at Daniel, eyebrows quirked up. "Does that happen often?"

Daniel's face was clouded, a deep scowl immediately setting in. "Never." He had already risen up from his chair, but then he hesitated and shut down his computer.

Before he could reach the door, Jace caught up to him

and asked, "Do you think your searches about Noah tipped him off?"

Daniel shook his head. "I barely got through my email."

They didn't speak on the walk up to the Colonel's office, which was apparently on the third floor in the far corner overlooking a manicured and spectacularly green lawn.

Daniel paused before knocking on the door. "Let me do the talking. We don't want to give anything away if we don't have to."

Jace just nodded. Whatever the family dynamics were, he was certain Daniel knew them better than he did.

Daniel knocked on the door but didn't wait for permission—he just strode in, full of sudden confidence, as if he was marching into a gladiator ring and needed to wear all of his courage in his bristled-out stance. It telegraphed his alpha-ness in a very obvious way. Daniel was younger than him by at least five years, but any shifter with military training had their alpha nature fully emerged by the time they graduated boot camp. The River pack was filled with military wolves, each of whom could easily have their own pack. It was part of what made the River pack strong, the willingness of so many alpha males to submit to the one pack alpha, his brother, Jaxson. It was also the reason why so many of the local packs came to them when they had some kind of problem with the shifter world. Or even the non-shifter world.

Daniel approached his father's huge oak desk with his shoulders thrown back and his head held high. "You wished to see me, sir?"

Daniel's father didn't look up from his phone, ignoring their entrance, a move clearly meant to put Daniel in his place. The Colonel's desk was lined with several crystalline-etched awards, each prominently displaying his name—Lt. Col. Astor Wilding. The metals decorating the Colonel's chest were likewise prominent. Which was even more obnoxious, given the dress code throughout the building was regulation desert camouflage, as far as Jace could tell.

The Colonel looked like he was ready for a parade of one.

Jace disliked him immediately. And not just a casual dislike, either. It was a visceral sort of thing, deep in his gut—his wolf was reacting to a presence it had identified as *the enemy*. Not just another alpha wolf—that wouldn't raise this kind of instinctual wariness. Somehow his wolf knew the Colonel was a destructive force, like a hurricane—inherently uncontrolled and dangerous, with the power to destroy everything in its path.

Astor Wilding finally looked up from his phone. He stayed seated. "I hear you lost your identification, Daniel."

"Temporarily misplaced it." Daniel stood rigidly under the patronizing smirk from his father. "I'm sure it'll turn up soon. Just needed some temporary ID to get on base and back to work."

Colonel Wilding eased up from his chair, slowly and casually, as if this little meeting hadn't been called by him. He strolled around to the front of his desk with the coiled strength of a shifter, but somehow it was more *predatory* than Jace had seen most wolves display. He'd known a few dark wolves in his time—men who let their dark human natures corrupt the wolf inside—but even they didn't have this sort of controlled menace built into their every move. It reminded Jace of the sinuous way that witches moved—not the sweet and innocent kind, like Olivia, but more like her coven sisters. The ones who liked to eat wolf hearts for breakfast. Or other body parts.

The Colonel trailed his fingers along his desk as if

inspecting his many awards for dust and came to rest at the front. He leaned against it, regarding Daniel with a look that made Jace's stomach clench. It boggled his mind that this was Daniel's *father*—and Colonel Wilding was looking at his son as if he was an enemy he'd like to torture, piece by bloody piece.

"Would you like to know where your identification turned up, Daniel?" the Colonel asked. "You might find it amusing."

"Yes, sir." Daniel's flat voice gave nothing away.

Jace felt like he was watching a chess match in operation.

"Turns out your security codes were swiped at 0600 this morning. By a young woman named Daniela Wuldinger." Astor folded his arms across his substantially-decorated chest and waited for a response.

"Guards the gate getting a little lax, are they?" Daniel's voice seemed uncertain, even to Jace, but his father rose to the weakness like a lion sensing the weakest member of the herd.

"Are you really going to stand there and tell me you had no idea your sister took your ID?" The laugh in the Colonel's voice said that punishment was guaranteed, but the severity of it was riding on Daniel's answer.

He hesitated.

Jace had to bite back the words on the tip of his tongue. *No, asshole, he knew. He was trying to protect her from* you. A cold trickle through Jace's belly told him something was very off about this—like Astor Wilding knew far more about this than they did.

Daniel's lack of an answer dragged on. He was obviously struggling for words that would thread him through the landmines his father had laid.

Jace cringed on Daniel's behalf, and it was all he could do to keep quiet.

Finally, Daniel said, "I knew she had the ID." His shoulders dropped a little. Those words were some kind of defeat.

His father nodded, a cruel smirk creeping onto his face. "I'll deal with you in a moment, son." The Colonel turned to Jace. "And *you…* exactly why has one of the River brothers decided to pay a visit to my base?"

*To tell you to fuck off in person?* Jace was surprised how violent his feelings were in such a short period of time around this man. His wolf may be locked away, but his instincts still ran strong.

Jace stepped forward, so that he was now standing slightly in front of Daniel. "Your son was an instrumental part of a rescue mission my brothers and I were involved in," he said, holding the Colonel's narrow-eyed glare without flinching. Daniel was having convulsions of body language, trying to tell Jace to shut up. Jace ignored him and took a step closer to the Colonel, moving into his space. "Those were *civilian* shifters, snatched off the street. One was a little girl from *your own pack*, in case you hadn't heard." His wolf was climbing up with his anger, so he tried to cool it down. "And now I hear military shifters are going missing."

If the Colonel's expression was menacing before, his look now sharpened to outright deadly, but his voice was cool and even. "Speaking of rumors… you used to be Army, didn't you? Medical Specialist Jace River, honorably discharged. At least, that's the official report. *I hear* there are rumors of something much less… *honorable* that happened in Afghanistan. But we wouldn't want to believe all the rumors we hear, now would we, Mr. River?"

*Shit.* That long delay at processing suddenly made sense—this guy researched the hell out of him since he walked in the gate. "What exactly are you threatening me with, Col. Wilding?" Jace's throat was so tight he had to growl the words out. The official tribunal had ruled the incident an accident, but Jace and his wolf knew the truth. Did the Colonel?

The man smirked, falling back into the ease he had before. "Not threatening a thing, Mr. River. Just saying, one shouldn't always believe the tall tales one might hear. Especially from my daughter."

Jace's mouth dropped open, but he snapped it shut again. "You have Piper."

The Colonel leaned back, tapped his phone, and said, "Bring her in."

Jace just blinked at the smirking satisfaction on the man's face. He had Piper all this time but played these games with them instead. It would be one thing if it were just Jace, but he wasn't even the primary target for the Colonel's aggression... that would be his son, Daniel, who seemed to have lost all the blood in his face.

The door swung open, and Piper stumbled in with two Military Police right behind her. The MPs were either shifters or bulked up like ones... and they had clearly been holding her tightly by the arm in the hallway. Jace could still see the imprint of their meaty hands on her wrinkled, white blouse. She defiantly glared at the Colonel and pursed her lips when her gaze fell on Daniel, but when her eyes finally found Jace... her expression went blank with surprise.

Jace wanted to go to her side, but she wasn't free yet. He swung back to the Colonel. Daniel was standing next to him, mute and blinking. He was waiting for the Colonel to mete out whatever his punishment was going to be... for all of them.

*Fuck that.* "On what grounds are you holding her?" Jace demanded. He needed more information to find a way to get her out of her father's clutches.

"Holding her?" Colonel Wilding asked with amusement in his eyes. "I was about to have her escorted from the base. Is there some reason why I should keep her in custody, Mr. River?"

Jace narrowed his eyes at the man. What games was he playing? "So... she's free to go?"

The Colonel ignored him and flicked a dismissive hand at Daniel, who jumped with the motion. "Get her out of here. If I see her on my base again, she'll do time. And I'll hold you *personally* responsible, Daniel."

Daniel visibly swallowed, gritted his teeth, and strode toward the door. Piper's expression of burning hatred was back and aimed at her father, who was busy returning his attention to his phone on the other side of his desk and completely ignoring her.

Daniel grabbed her by the upper arm and leaned close. "Let's go," he hissed.

She let out something like a growl, then allowed Daniel to haul her into the hallway outside her father's office. The MPs followed, clearly intent on escorting them out with their hulking presence. Jace hurried after them.

Daniel and Piper kept an angry silence on the way downstairs and toward the front of the building, no doubt because the MPs would overhear, but Piper flicked a couple looks back to Jace, trailing behind, with something like amazement in her eyes. He wasn't quite sure what that was about, but he *really* wanted to ask her what went down before she got caught. They would have time for that later. Besides, there was an undeniable relief coursing through his system at seeing her unharmed and knowing she was on her way to freedom. Although, he really had no idea *how* that had happened.

Just as they were about to exit the building, Jace felt a hot sensation on the back of his neck—it was the prickling feeling you got when someone was watching you. He whipped his gaze around the two-story entranceway they were striding through… and just barely caught a glimpse of someone ducking back inside one of the offices at the perimeter of the white-granite-lined open space. A hot surge of anger froze him in his tracks.

*Agent Smith.*

Jace could have sworn it was him, but he was gone now. Jace started to trot toward the office, intent on catching whoever it was and seeing if it was really the asshole who had been capturing and torturing shifters, including little girls, but a voice stopped him cold.

"Hold it right there, sir!" One of the MPs had his weapon out, pointed at Jace's head.

He put up his hands and turned to face the MP. "Just had to use the restroom before we left."

*"No, sir."* His aim was unwavering. "My orders are to escort all three of you off the base."

Jace grimaced, but there wasn't anything to be done about it. They were on the Colonel's turf, and they were lucky to be staying out of the brig.

"All right, fine. No need to get excited." He lowered his hands and took his time strolling over to where Daniel and Piper waited with the second MP at the entrance door. Daniel looked like he was barely keeping from shifting, with the livid anger on his face, and Piper was working hard, too… to keep a smirk contained.

"Bathroom break?" she asked quietly as they trotted

down the steps to the parking lot below.

"Hey, when nature calls, a guy's gotta go." He gave her a small smile.

She chuckled under her breath, then gave the MPs a final glare before climbing into the back of Daniel's car.

The MPs followed them in a military police car all the way to the entrance of the base.

# CHAPTER 6

To Piper's utter amazement, she was riding in the back of Daniel's car, free as a bird, leaving the Joint Base instead of heading to the brig. Or FBI custody. Even more amazingly, Jace River sat in the passenger seat, giving her an occasional smirk over his shoulder. By unspoken agreement—probably because all three of them were holding their breath—they waited until they were through the gate and off base, leaving the MPs behind, before speaking.

"You really know how to screw things up, don't you, Piper?" Daniel's voice was tight.

At least his opinion was no surprise. "It wasn't exactly part of my plan to get caught."

"Oh, I guess that makes it better." Daniel's scowl reached across the seat and smothered her words of indignation before they could fly out of her mouth. "At least now we know there are no missing soldiers."

"Um… you do realize that was complete bullshit, right?" Jace looked at Daniel like he couldn't quite believe he would be that naïve. But he didn't know her brother like Piper did. Daniel only saw what he wanted to.

Daniel flicked his scowl between Piper and Jace.

She fought to wipe the grin from her face. It was amazing that Jace was here at all, much less defending her against Daniel—it brought a delightfully unfamiliar feeling of having someone actually in her corner. Add on top that Jace was helping her get off base without being arrested or held for questioning, and he was officially her favorite shifter at the moment. But something wasn't right about all of this—in fact, she had no idea why her father let her go.

While Daniel was still struggling to understand what Jace meant, Piper captured his gaze. "Why are you helping me?"

"I told you before," Jace said, "I'm not leaving a fellow grunt behind." His slight smile was inscrutable as he looked her over. "Are you sure you're okay?"

"I'm fine." Piper grimaced—the MPs had a bit of fun with her dignity, shoving her around and leering at her when her father wasn't present. Not that it would have mattered if he had been—he'd done far worse to her himself back when she was still living in his house. Never outright physical or sexual abuse, just the mental kind. And the MPs didn't harm her beyond the bruises from the cuffs and a sore shoulder from when they'd thrown her to the ground, then yanked her back up again. As if she'd done anything close to resisting arrest.

Besides, she would take a beating any day—it had happened a couple times in the field when she'd messed up, not been careful enough—rather than endure the cutting words that came out of her father's mouth. Somehow, with a single, carefully placed sneer, the Colonel could reduce her to that eight-year-old who innocently asked him why he didn't love her. He'd told her in military-precise terms why she wasn't worthy of his love. The Colonel favored his sons over her, but he was really a monster to everyone—he'd branded Daniel and

Noah each with a special kind of abuse. She could still see the emotional scars plastered across Daniel's face, even though he'd never admit to it. When both Noah and Daniel were sent overseas, she breathed a sigh of relief just to have them out of the Colonel's zone of influence. Noah saw their father for what he truly was, but somehow, Daniel never did.

Piper must have been subconsciously rubbing the bruises on her wrists because Jace was scowling in spite of her assurances that she was fine.

"What did they do to you?" he asked. There was an audible growl in his voice.

She growled right back. "I told you, I'm fine."

Even Daniel looked concerned now, throwing a glance over the seat at her and scanning her body for signs of injury or something, instead of watching the road.

"Eyes forward," she said, but without too much harshness. "I am *not* going to die on a side street in Washington just because you forgot how to drive." Her sass didn't seem to deter their concerned looks. She sighed. "Look, they just cuffed me a little more roughly than necessary. It's nothing. Trust me, I've seen a lot worse in the field."

That seemed to reassure Daniel, but Jace's expression just darkened further. What was his deal? Why was he even here? She wasn't sure she bought this whole *rescuing all the shifters* thing. Was anyone really that heroic?

"I don't understand why the Colonel let you go." Daniel's voice had returned to his normal mode of disapproval.

"Would you rather he turned me over to the FBI?" she asked, her ire rising again. "Thanks, bro."

"I'm just saying, it just doesn't make sense." He scowled at her again.

Jace twisted around to face her, his eyes alight with curiosity. "How far did you get?" He still had that rough, just-tumbled-out-of-bed look, and her wolf responded to that direct gaze more than she would have liked.

"What do you mean?" she asked, trying to recover from the sudden flush of lust. For God's sake, she didn't even understand why he was here. Or why a single, piercing look from him was enough to set her nether parts on fire.

Jace gave her a small smile. "I'm assuming you earned the cuffing. What did you find out before you were caught?"

She huffed a short laugh. Was he flirting with her?

"Actually, I didn't get far. Couldn't even access the central database. They must have known I had a false ID from the jump and just waited to see what I was up to before nabbing me."

Jace nodded. "Makes sense. Which begs the question of why they let you go. It's not like falsifying classified access ID isn't a crime, you know."

Piper shrugged one shoulder, and Jace looked like he was holding back a smirk.

Daniel had no humor on his face whatsoever. "Once again, you get off scot-free," he grumbled. "And I'm going to pay for this, one way or another."

Piper sighed. Her father probably *would* punish Daniel for letting her lift his credentials, even though it wasn't his fault. It would never cross the Colonel's mind to consider who might actually be at fault in a situation— he'd only care about how he could use it to his advantage.

"If I were you," Piper said. "I'd work on getting deployed again. Safer in Afghanistan."

Daniel snorted his agreement—they both knew the score on that much, at least, even if Daniel was more than willing to heap the blame on *her* all the time, for everything. But they both knew from personal experience that dodging bullets for your country was preferable to an extended stay stateside in the sphere of influence of their father.

It was Jace's turn to seem baffled.

Piper turned to him. "I'm sure my father has his own reasons for letting me go, but it's also possible one of my superiors stepped in. I need to check in with the office as soon as possible." She didn't mention she had no intention of telling them anything they didn't already know. This could be entirely her father playing some game where she didn't even know the players on the board, much less the game map or the rules. Part of why she was good at her job was having grown up in a house full of secrets and lies.

Jace nodded and turned to the front, a puzzled look still on his face.

They kept quiet for the rest of the hour-long drive back to the safehouse, each immersed in their own thoughts. Piper had no incentive to explain anything, not until she had a better handle on why Jace was helping her. Maybe he was genuinely concerned about Noah. The River brothers' pack had that gung-ho attitude, for sure—they did help out with rescuing Cassie after all.

Her bad guy radar was telling her Jace was one of the good guys. Her wolf had been desperately panting after him since the moment he showed up, and it would be nice to think he was helping out because he liked that hot kiss in the kitchen as much as she did. But coming after her at the Joint Base? That was a lot of risk to take, and Piper was sure someone as hot as Jace River didn't have to work that hard for a bed partner. There was more to it than that, but she didn't have a handle on it yet. And Piper didn't like things she didn't understand. It made her twitchy—not knowing what was happening was a good way to get strung up in a Nicaraguan warehouse in the jungle. She'd had enough of *that* for a lifetime.

When they arrived at the safehouse, Piper was surprised to see how busy it was. The place was filled to the rafters with shifters, mostly male and definitely hot. She was swimming in male flesh once again, all of it shifter. Her wolf was going nuts.

There were a few females as well, and Jace quickly introduced her to his mother, who met them at the door. She had gorgeous silver hair with streaks of white flowing in long waves to her waist. If Piper didn't know better, she would've thought Mama River was a witch, with her regal beauty and slender limbs. Piper certainly hadn't expected the warm hug and hadn't returned it at all. Then, suddenly, she was being ushered into the kitchen.

A strange sense of guilt washed over her as Jace's mother shoved a plateful of gorgeous-looking pastries, fruits, and cheeses at her, along with the giant glass of milk. The guilt turned into a vague sense of being insulted—Mama River was treating Piper like a child—but it was obvious that this was the warm sort of childhood Jace and his brothers had. The kind she never did. She was a giant bag of emotions over this—the sense of insult and guilt was now being thrashed with a heavy dose of envy—but it was all quickly washed away by a flush of craving. The food beckoned, her stomach growled, and there was no denying she was famished. Her 3 am adventures had stretched without a break into the afternoon of the next day.

Piper smiled at Mama River and dug into the food. Jace and his mother both had grins on their faces, although Jace's was a little more amused than pleased. Daniel seemed baffled that she had decided now was a good time to eat, but it wasn't like the Colonel had given her anything.

People wandered in and out of the kitchen, but they didn't take much notice of her tucked in the tiny eat-in table in the corner. After she spent a minute of blissful silence devouring the delicious treats, two shifters strode into the kitchen, trailed by a younger woman. It was obvious the men were related to Jace, only older: same towering, bulked-up bodies with a hardness that came from military service, not just the shifter gene; same intelligent eyes; same confident alpha walk. Their faces were all hard planes and kissable lips, but they also had a touch of the softness she saw in Mama River's open concern for her—it was like kindness personified, touching their faces with a glow that came from lives surrounded by people they loved.

One of the men glowed more than the others, the one with his fingers laced with the girl's. She was a curvy, dark-haired beauty, and anyone with eyes could see the man was madly in love with her.

"Hey," he said to Jace, "I've got some good news for you. But first, tell me—" He cut himself off as he noticed Piper at the table, scarfing down pastries. "Oh! You must be Piper." He dropped the girl's hand and strode over.

Piper regretfully put down the chocolate croissant she was about to devour and rose up from her chair. She didn't say anything, just tried to gauge his intention.

He extended his hand and a smile. "I'm Jaxson River. I hear you have a brother we're going to find."

Her heart couldn't help responding—a smile snuck on

her face without her permission. She shook his hand. "I hope so." The words came out more emotional than she intended, so she ducked her head and tried to get a grip on herself. She dropped his hand and backed up a little to gain space. The girl arrived at Jaxson's side.

"Hey, I'm Olivia." She offered up her small hand.

Piper leaned over to shake that, too, then retreated again. "Piper Wilding."

Olivia grinned. "We know. And I think I might be able to help you." She looked to Jaxson for confirmation, and he gave her an encouraging nod. She turned back to Piper. "You should know I'm half-witch."

Piper took a step back that banged her legs against the chair she'd just been seated in.

"It's okay." Olivia's hands were up. "I'm one of the nice ones."

"I didn't think they came in that flavor." Piper peered around her for the matriarch of the River pack, wondering if maybe *she* was a witch, too, as she appeared, but she had already slipped away.

"If you'd asked me last week," Olivia said with a smile, "I would have said the same thing. I didn't think witches could be anything but nasty and evil." She beamed a newlywed look at Jaxson. "But then I fell in love with a wolf, and that kind of changed my perspective."

Piper frowned. "You two are mated?" She'd never heard of such a thing. In fact, she wasn't even sure it was possible.

"Mated, in love, and soon to be married," Jaxson said with a grin that implied this was still a brand-spanking-new turn of events, and he wasn't tired of boasting about it yet.

"Um... congratulations?" Piper couldn't quite wrap her head around the details, but that wasn't really her concern, anyway.

Olivia gave Jaxson's arm an affectionate squeeze, and Piper was suddenly spiked through with envy for the second time in less than five minutes—not only did these River wolves grow up with a family that obviously loved them, but they had mates who adored them as well. Her heart twitched, wondering if Jace had a mate, and she flashed a look to him.

He was watching her carefully, like he was studying her every small movement, and she had to wrench her gaze away before her thoughts were betrayed on her face. Even if Olivia was a witch, that clearly didn't stand in the way of her and Jaxson falling in love. In fact, their love must be pretty epic to bridge that kind of gulf. All Piper had was a damaged childhood and a series of anonymous orgasms.

Her whole body stiffened. It didn't matter if Jace River had a mate, because *she*—Piper Wilding—had long ago vowed never to take one. A vow her wolf was objecting to more with each passing moment. Clearly, Piper needed to limit her time at the River family safehouse. Ten minutes in, and it was already causing massive internal chaos.

"Never mind all that," said Olivia. "What matters is that, even though I'm half witch and seriously out of practice using magic, I have something that might help you. I just spent the morning with my Aunt Gwen learning a seeking spell. If you would like, I can try to find your brother, Noah."

Piper blinked and took a moment to respond. "You can do that?"

Olivia nodded.

"I… um…" Her brain was spinning with this. "Will it hurt him in some way?" Piper really had no idea how witches did their magic. Everything she had heard about witches involved bloody death, pack-wide destruction, and general painful mayhem.

"Oh no! It won't hurt him at all. But I will need your assistance. And it might be a little… embarrassing? I don't know what kind of relationship you have with your brother." She glanced at Daniel, who suddenly looked extremely uncomfortable. Olivia looked back to Piper. "I'll have to access some of your memories of him so the spell can hone in on his trace in the magical world. Would that be all right?"

Piper nodded quickly. "I have no problem with that, not if it will help us find him."

"Great." Jaxson looked to Jace. "Did you have any luck at the base in figuring out where Noah might be?"

Jace gave a quick look to Piper, but all he said was, "No."

Then Jaxson turned to the third River brother. "Jared, what about your facial recognition search at Riverwise? Anything on Agent Smith there?"

"Nothing so far, but I'm running a few new algorithms. Would be better if we had a picture of the guy, not just my sketch. My art skills kind of suck." Jared was a bit gruff, but Piper liked him immediately. Seemed like an all-business kind of guy, not quite as soft as the others. She appreciated that. Although as far as her wolf was concerned, even with hot shifters wandering in and out of the kitchen every minute, there was really only one man in the room—and Jace was still watching her with the kind of piercing intensity that made her think he was taking notes on her every word and move.

He broke his inspection of her to glance at his older brother. "I might actually have something on the Agent Smith front. When I was at the base, I saw someone I'm pretty sure was him. I don't know what he was doing there, but I don't believe in that kind of coincidence. We already know he's working for some part of the government, and now with military shifters disappearing? I don't like it, Jaxson. Not at all."

"Agreed," Jaxson said. "It's just as well you got out of there."

"Wait a minute, who is this Agent Smith person?" Piper asked. Was that who Jace tried to go back for? And why didn't he bring it up sooner?

"He's the bad guy responsible for the other shifters who were kidnaped, including Cassie," Jace explained.

Piper nodded, forgiving him for the moment—at least they were after the same bad guys. Piper turned back to Olivia. "All right, what do I have to do for this spell? I don't know anything about this Agent Smith, I just want to find my brother. But it sounds like, if we can do that, we might find any other shifters involved in this thing. Because I can't believe it's just my brother. There has to be more to it than that."

Jace stepped forward. "I agree," he said softly, but full of meaning. "If we work together, we'll have a much better chance of solving this whole thing. Including finding Noah."

So maybe that was it. He came after her because he believed she had vital information that could help him and the rest of his brothers find the missing shifters and this Agent Smith character. It wasn't that he was *worried* about her or any such nonsense.

"Understood." She was a little disappointed it wasn't more than that, but that helped focus her back on her mission: *finding Noah.*

Jaxson tugged on Jace's arm, pulling him back to give Piper and Olivia room. Olivia produced a small baggie filled with whitish powder from the pocket of her jeans. She poured it out into the palm of her hand and waved her other hand over it. She said some strange words in a hesitating kind of way, like she didn't quite know what they were. *Great.* A beginner half-witch. But the spell must be working because a whitish cloud started to swirl above the tiny pile of powder. Blue sparks shot through the cloud, forming a little torrent of magic.

"Are you ready?" Olivia looked her in the eyes, little more uncertainty there than Piper wanted to see.

"Um… sure." Piper braced herself, but the last thing she expected was for Olivia to blow the small cloud into her face. The world went blurry at the edges, and Piper tried not to panic. She clutched at the table top next to her, bracing herself as her vision wobbled. All the shifters in the room seemed to blur like she was seeing them from underwater.

Olivia's voice boomed, suddenly loud like she was in a giant hall. "Focus on your brother, Noah, and some particularly poignant memory that you have. The stronger, the better."

A dozen memories flashed through Piper's head, mostly text conversations that were particularly funny or sad. There was something about communicating by typed words on her phone that allowed her and Noah to share things they never could face-to-face. In fact, there was literally no one else on earth she would say those things to, even in a text. But even as strong as those memories were, they still wobbled away from her, like her mind was searching for something more tangible. Something in person.

Her thoughts suddenly zoomed all the way back to the day their mother died. Piper's mind snapped to the on-base housing that was more like a prison. Her mother had always stayed in the house. The Colonel liked it that way and forbade her from showing her beautiful face outside its four walls. There was something about the mating bond that held her captive. The one time Piper had tried to get her mother to leave—for some school function or play date or normal thing of childhood she couldn't even recall now—her mother had something akin to a panic attack. Piper never asked again. That was when her mother's slow descent started. Piper could see it in retrospect, but at the time, she just thought her mom was sick a lot.

Then that day came when Piper came home late from school. Even before she was halfway across the living room, she knew something had gone terribly wrong. Noah stormed out of the kitchen, eyes red, face streaked with tears, so angry-looking that Piper thought he might explode. Or shift. Something. But Noah kept his rage locked inside, even then, just as they had all learned to do.

*"What happened?"* she remembered asking. Noah just shook his head, the rage making his whole body vibrate.

It wasn't until Piper stumbled into the kitchen herself that she understood. Her mother was sprawled out on the kitchen floor. A bottle of pills had spilled across the kitchen table, and a bottle of whiskey had smashed into the floor, spilling its amber liquid into a thin lake that stretched across the span of the kitchen.

Piper remembered that she screamed. She didn't remember actually doing it, but her throat was sore for days afterward. There was no sense in calling 911 because it was obvious her mother was dead.

Noah had been the first to discover her body.

"Oh my God, Piper, I'm so sorry." Olivia's voice resonated through the vision like a sonic boom and wiped it away.

Piper's body was rigid—bound up from the vision—but with Olivia's words, everything drained from her. The room spun, still blurry at the edges, and she almost went down.

Suddenly, Jace was holding her up, his dark, concerned eyes peering down at her and his strong arms keeping her upright. She allowed herself to sag into him—it was either that or end up on the floor—and as her head thumped against his chest, she said, "Please tell me that worked. I don't think I can do it again."

His arms were tight around her, holding her up, but he twisted toward Olivia.

"I've got him!" she said triumphantly.

# CHAPTER 7

Jace held Piper close—she still seemed woozy from the seeking spell Olivia cast to find her brother, but that wasn't the only reason he was holding her. *She needed him.* He felt it deep in his core, and there was no way he was letting go of that... or her. But once Olivia's claim of having magically found Noah seemed to register, Piper gently pushed him away. She wobbled a little, but managed to stay upright on her own.

"What did you see?" Piper asked Olivia.

Olivia reached for Piper's hand and squeezed it, but she quickly pulled back and crossed her arms tightly across her chest. She was locking herself in again, walling herself off from anyone and everyone who tried to help her.

"I saw your brother in a hospital," Olivia said. "It looked more like a military hospital, with guys in fatigues with guns. Noah was lying on a thin cot. There were others too."

"How many?" Jace asked.

Piper frowned at his question, but he couldn't figure out why.

"About a dozen I think," Olivia answered. "It was hard to tell. The windows around the edges of the long ward were dark, and the overhead lights were dim."

"It was dark outside?" Piper asked. The afternoon light shone brightly out the window of the kitchen. "Are you saying this was a vision of the future? I thought this was a seeking spell."

Olivia frowned. "I'm not exactly sure what I saw. Maybe the past?" She bit her lip. "But I can tell you exactly where it was."

"You can?" Jace asked, skeptically. "How does that work?"

Olivia shrugged. "It's hard to explain, but it's like a witchy GPS. All I know is, if you give me a map, I can point to the exact location of my vision. I'm sorry, I'm still new at this."

"It's better than any lead I've had so far." Piper leaned forward to squeeze Olivia's hand, then quickly retreated again.

"I'll pull up a map," Jaxson said, grabbing a tablet from a nearby kitchen counter and tapping it open. "Jared, gather up a few of our pack and get them ready to head out."

Jace lifted his chin to catch Jared's attention. "We won't know the situation until we get there, but we shouldn't need more than five or six total. Keep it small."

Jared nodded his agreement and hustled out of the room.

Jace looked back to Piper. Her pretty face was still pale and grim. "Are you all right?"

"Yeah, I'll be okay."

She didn't look okay, but his words seem to lift her a little. He didn't know what happened in the seeking spell, but it shook her. Badly. Whatever it was just reinforced that sense he had that she was fragile right now, whether she wanted to acknowledge that or not. And that she needed his support.

The trick would be getting her to let him.

He smiled at her, putting all the reassurance into it that he could. It seemed to affect her: she ducked her head and braced herself against the table, making it look casual, but he could see the unsteadiness behind it. He didn't know what it would take to break down those walls—the ones that kept everyone out—but he was surprised by his own determination to find out.

Jerod quickly returned with three pack members in tow, and they all piled into the safehouse van. Daniel came along as well, and of course, Piper insisted on coming. That got a few frowns from the rest of the pack, but he glared them down. Asking her to stay home from the mission would just drive her away—he knew that much. And he suspected she had as much, if not more, experience with this sort of thing than they did. Olivia stayed behind; she'd already helped enough, and Jaxson wouldn't risk her on a mission, even if they could use her help.

Piper rode in silence, one giant ball of tension. Daniel had a permanent scowl on his face. Jace didn't know what his take on this was, but he seemed willing to go along and see if they could actually find his brother.

When they were nearly there, Daniel checked his phone—his scowl grew even deeper.

"What's up?" Piper asked. They were the first words she'd spoken during the trip.

Daniel hesitated to answer, then said, "I just got an email from Noah."

"*What?*" Piper rose half out of her seat, but then slumped back down with the jostling of the van. "What does it say?"

Daniel held up his phone and read the email aloud. "Hey, Daniel, I heard you were worried about me. Wanted to let you know I was fine. Just taking a little time to relax. I'll be back up to speed in no time. Don't worry about me. Stay cool, bro."

Daniel and Piper exchanged a look, and both of them seemed freaked out by the email, but Jace couldn't figure out what was wrong with it. "So… what? Is he really okay?"

Piper shook her head, and Daniel seem to agree, but he was scanning the email again.

"He said *back up to speed.*" Piper's voice was filled with dread. "That's what we said when we were kids after…" She glanced around the crowded van. Jace was sure she didn't want to spill whatever personal family secret this was amongst a bunch of shifters she didn't know.

"After something bad happened," Jace filled in for her.

She looked relieved and sent him a grateful look. "Yes. If he really wanted to say he was fine, he would've said something more like *I'm dying of dysentery, but I'm sure I'll be over it in a few months. If not, don't get weepy at my funeral.*"

Jace only knew a little about her family and the asshole who was their father, but he could imagine the level of gallows humor was pretty intense. "So his email is code for *something's really bad.* Like in Olivia's vision with the hospital beds?"

Piper just nodded.

Daniel's jaw was tight. "Should I answer this?"

"Leave it for now." Jace glanced up front to the driver, who gave him a nod in the rearview mirror. "We're almost there."

They piled out of the van. This dark corner of Seattle was filled with rusted out warehouses and abandoned buildings.

Jaxson brought out the GPS and pointed down the road. "It's about three blocks that way. I think we should send an advanced scout. Jace?"

He nodded his agreement. "I'll take Piper, and we'll signal back with a text once we've checked out the situation. If we need to plan a larger assault, we might have to wait until dark and call up some reinforcements." Jace reached for Piper's hand, but she was already heading off in the direction of the warehouse or hospital or whatever this place was. He gave a small shrug to Jaxson's questioning look and jogged after her.

When he caught up, he said, "You know, we've done a few operations like this before. You might want to use some of our expertise and not just always run off by yourself. More likely to achieve success in our mission objectives that way." He tried to keep his voice light, but in order to get her brother and the others out alive, she needed to not go off half-cocked.

She checked her pace. "I really do appreciate your help. I'm just used to working alone."

It made him cringe—he had a feeling *alone* was what she felt most of the time. "I know. But we're in this together now, right?"

"Sure." It was the most negative form of a *yes* that Jace had ever heard.

He just shook his head. His GPS showed them approaching the coordinates—the target was just another rusty warehouse like all the others. Jace tugged Piper around the corner, out of view of the building. Then he peeked around and took a quick scan.

"Not seeing any movement," he said.

She did a peek-check as well. "I think we need to get closer. Those low windows could give us a preview of what's waiting inside." She gave him the most honest look he'd ever seen from her. "We need to be careful. If they're in hospital beds, it might be hard to move them. We need to count the guards, assess the weapons, and make a plan to take them all out at once. Give us time to move the prisoners."

He gave her a small smile. "You know, I could use someone like you on my other missions." Not only was it true, it made him want to shove her up against the wall and kiss the hell out of her. Which really wasn't appropriate at the moment. "I don't suppose you'd consider joining the pack?"

She rolled her eyes. "Are you kidding me? You guys don't have near as much fun in your jobs as I do."

He snorted a laugh. "All right, we do this your way. I'll take one of the near windows, you take one closer to the door. Get a peek-check, then reconvene back here. Acceptable?"

She smirked. "I can work with that."

They split up, crouching low and running fast. The thrill of being on a mission with her was getting his wolf way too excited—it kept trying to claw its way up from the depths. Jace reached his window at the same time Piper reached hers, and with a coordinated signal between them, they both peek-checked at the same time, then ducked back down below the window. What he saw was not encouraging. By the frown on Piper's face, she'd seen the same thing.

*Nothing.*

There were hospital beds inside the building all right, but no people whatsoever. Jace stood and peered in the window again; Piper did the same. Then she slammed her fist against the side of the window, making it rattle. Jace jogged over to her, pulling out his phone to text his brothers and the rest of the pack. He quickly tapped out the message: *hospital here, no prisoners.* Then he stowed his phone in his pocket again.

"I'm going inside," Piper ground out. She stormed off toward the door a dozen feet away. It was locked. She banged on it and yanked the handle, then finally whipped out some claws and sliced through the thin sheet metal with a screeching sound that echoed down the street.

Jace rushed over to her. "Piper—" But she'd already reached through the door, unlocked it, and yanked it open, rushing inside.

He quickly followed. She dashed along the two rows of hospital beds, stopping at each one to throw back the blankets and check for something, then moving on to the next. About halfway down the long open space, she scooped up something and froze.

Jace finally caught up to her. "What is it?"

She had an envelope in her hands, but she was just staring at it. "If Noah had been here, he would've left some clue for me. He knows I would come looking for him."

Jace nodded. If one of his brothers were in trouble, Jace would do the same, looking for them tirelessly. And he would expect them to help by leaving clues along the way. As messed up as Piper's family was, he had no doubt that the bond between Piper and Noah was just as strong.

"Why don't you open it?" he asked.

She flipped open the flap to show him—the envelope was empty.

"An empty envelope? What does it mean?" He frowned—it wasn't much of a clue.

She looked at him with one of those hard looks that he didn't like, like she was churning through her mind whether she could trust Jace enough to tell him the truth.

"I'm here to help you, Piper," he said gently.

She nodded. "It's not what's inside, it's the envelope itself." She took his hand and ran one of his fingers along the back flap. It had a slightly raised embossing. When Jace looked more closely, could see an emblem: some kind of eagle and flag, barely visible.

"It's some kind of official US government envelope," Jace said, still not really understanding. "How does that help?"

"It's the official stationery of Senator Krepky's office in the capitol." Piper's voice was flat.

"You think one of the Senators is involved in this?" Jace suspected it was a government operation, but he couldn't believe the politicians would get their hands muddy with any of it.

"I'm going to find out." Piper stuffed the envelope into her jacket pocket and turned to stride away.

"Hang on!" Jace reached out to tug on her elbow and stop her from leaving. "We're sticking together, remember? Let me help you with this."

At that exact moment, the rest of the pack stormed

into the building, weapons out, fanning to check every nook and corner to see if someone was lurking there. Jaxson was in the lead. He quickly gave the all clear signal to his pack and hurried up to Jace and Piper.

His brother scowled at him. "Empty warehouse. Recently evacuated. Last time I was in this situation, it went south pretty badly."

He was right, of course—the last time they found a supposedly empty warehouse, when they were trying to rescue their brother, Jared, it turned out to be Agent Smith's trap to capture them all.

Jace tugged Piper closer, his hand still on her elbow. "Jaxson's right. We shouldn't stay here. Let's head out and make our plans from there."

Jaxson signaled to the rest of the pack to head out of the building again. Daniel stayed behind. He and Piper exchanged some kind of look Jace didn't understand.

"This is all smoke and mirrors, Piper," Daniel said coldly. "Father's playing some kind of game with us."

"This isn't a game!" Piper shot back, her body going rigid with tension again.

"Noah isn't here," Daniel said. "There's no evidence he or any other shifters were *ever* here. The only actual evidence we have is an email that says he's fine."

"You know that's not what he meant." Piper's dark eyes were on fire with anger.

Daniel dismissed that with a wave. "I'm going back to work. If I still have a job after what you pulled this morning. You can chase your fantasies all you like, Piper." Then he turned on his heel and stormed out of the warehouse, fists clenched.

Jace looked at Piper, but she was too busy burning holes in Daniel's back to notice. "Ignore him. Trust your instincts on this. But we need to get out of here. We can't help your brother if we get caught in an ambush."

She gave him a sharp nod, and they headed out after the rest of the pack, giving Daniel wide berth. But as soon as they were clear of the door, Piper pulled off to the side, heading in the opposite direction.

"Where you going?" Jace turned to trot after her.

She stopped and let him catch up. "I'm going to figure out what happened to Noah."

"Maybe it's not the Senator. This looks military to me." Jace tried to soften his voice and reached for her arm, but she pulled away. "Is it possible your dad is involved? Agent Smith was on his turf. There's a connection there somehow."

"I'm following the clue Noah left for me."

Determination was a cold fire in her eyes.

"We can get the witches to help again," Jace tried.

She scowled. "Your witch is a novice."

"She'll get closer this time. At least give it a chance. If you take off again, how am I going to convince the pack you're not just a loose cannon?"

"I'm sure you can be convincing when you want to be." Then she reached up and grabbed his cheeks and pulled him down to kiss her. It was hot and fast, her tongue demanding a response from his, and he was crushing her body to his before he knew what he was doing. Just as lightning fast, she pulled back and smirked at him.

When he tried to bring her close again, she just pulled further out of reach.

"You're just trying to distract me," Jace said, breath already heavy from that one kiss. He wiped the taste of her off his lips with the back of his hand—not that he exactly minded that method of distraction.

Her smirk grew wider. "Yes."

"Is arguing just foreplay for you?" He was hoping that *foreplay* meant there would eventually be *more play*, but mostly he wanted to keep her from running off to do some dangerous solo mission again.

"Yes." Her smirk was so flirtatious now, it was all he could do not to force her up against the wall and give her a dose of her own medicine.

"It's not going to work," he said instead.

Her smile tempered a little. "The distraction or the foreplay part?"

"The distraction." This time, he did move a little closer. Maybe he could kiss his way into convincing her to stay.

She looked him up and down in a way that made his wolf surge up—and the man in him wanted to do all kinds of naughty things, right here, right now, forget the rest of the pack. They were all headed back to the van anyway.

Her roaming gaze finally found his eyes. "Where I need to go, you can't come. There's no way you can get into the Senator's office like I can."

*Dammit.* She was probably right about that. And yet he had absolutely no desire to let her go. "I don't like this, Piper."

"You don't have to." The warmth in her eyes cooled, like those brief moments of openness and flirtation had passed, and she was building up all her emotional walls again. Keeping him out; keeping him at a distance. She did it with everyone in her life. He'd only known her for a short time, but he'd already figured out that much.

He leaned in close, finally pushing her back against the rusty, corrugated wall of the warehouse, one hand on either side of her head. He was close enough to kiss, but instead he just whispered softly, "I want you to come back. Without handcuffs this time. Don't make me come rescue you again."

He thought she might kiss him, but the walls were already firmly back in place. And his words just conjured a cold fire in her eyes. She put both hands against his chest and shoved him away from her.

"I didn't need rescuing! I could've taken care of that myself. I don't need your help, Jace River. Or anyone else's." Then she wrenched away from him and stormed off.

Other than physically grabbing her and locking her in the van, he couldn't think of any way to stop her. He banged his head softly against the wall… and prayed she would make it back safely from whatever foolishness she was determined to do this time.

# CHAPTER 8

Piper hiked up the long stretch of white stone steps to the capitol building in Olympia. It had taken her over an hour to get there, but she could still feel Jace's lips on hers—that hot kiss outside the warehouse lingered long past the few seconds his mouth was actually on hers. It made her momentarily forget her brother had been kept inside that dingy medical prison, with people doing who knew what to him.

But she was back on point now.

The towering granite columns of the capitol building

were imposing to most people—they spoke of a stately elegance that was hilarious in the face of the smarmy politics that happened inside the building itself. Piper was a fan of democracy, but sometimes it was a wonder it could survive all the machinations of the politicians that made it run. It was certainly messy, and she had her hands in a fair share of the muck. Her work on the Senate Defense Subcommittee involved security issues and shifters—two things she knew quite a bit about—but she stayed away from the politics as much as possible. Her brother knew about her work, and he knew that envelope would point her directly here: Senator Krepky's office.

The gorgeous marble dome inside the capitol building soared above her, adding its regal gold-trimmed gleam to the interior. Piper waved to the guard manning the security checkpoint just inside the entranceway and swiped her credentials—the real ones that had top-level clearance for the Senate building. The guard gave her a warm smile return—he was the kind that remembered faces, and he always seemed to know hers, even with her somewhat infrequent but still regular visits to the capitol.

Once past security, she strode purposefully toward the Senator's office. She had already made an appointment with Michael, Krepky's personal assistant—getting an appointment with the Senator himself was quite difficult and completely unnecessary. Michael had access to all the Senator's top-secret information, the Senator's office, and he probably knew more about what was going on in the defense subcommittee than the Senator himself. The trick in counterintelligence was always to know where the true power resided—and Piper's radar for detecting the holders of power was as finely tuned as the radar she used to tell the good guys from the bad.

Jace River was definitely one of the good guys.

Her thoughts kept drifting back to him. She'd spent the entire car trip down to Olympia replaying that scorching kiss. She couldn't decide if Jace actually cared about her, for some strange reason, even though he had no reason at all. Just when she was convinced that he only cared about the mission, being a hero and rescuing other shifters, he went and did something like he did at the warehouse—not the kiss, but that soft whisper in her ear, saying that he wanted her to come back. Or asking her if she was okay once she was released from her father's custody. Or holding her when she felt woozy from the witch's spell that forced her to relive her mother's death. Piper doubted Jace had any idea the effect those things had on her—and she was little surprised herself at how quickly his small touches and concerned looks and hot kisses had reached inside her and stirred things around.

Whenever he smiled at her—and even worse, when he beamed that hot, smirky grin—it wasn't just her lady parts being warmed. The man was a hot shifter determined to help find her brother, and his kisses were like a drug for her inner beast. To top it all off, he seemed to actually care about her.

It was a deadly combination. And a dangerous one. It was seriously messing with her vow not to get involved, and certainly not to mate with, anyone, ever. Period. Full stop. It didn't matter how hot that shifter boy was or how much he wet her panties. Mating wasn't something she could even contemplate, not after what happened to her mom.

Piper needed to stay focused on her task, which right now included checking in with her office before she wound through the long corridors of the capitol to pay a visit to the Senator's minion. She needed to put out any fires at Civilian Defense and see if they knew about her infiltration of the Joint Base *before* meeting with Michael and doing what she had to do to uncover the Senator's involvement in all of this. She glanced down the hall to make sure it was clear, then paused by an alcove with a bust of a previous governor and dialed the number of the secure line for her office.

The call operator, Shelley, answered on the first ring. "Al's carpet installation, can I help you?"

Piper gave her access code, the 17 digit number that was her lifeline wherever she was in the world.

Shelley replied, "Piper! I was wondering when you were going to check in, girl. Your supervisor is not very pleased about your vacation plans."

So far, so good. "Yeah, well, looks like I'm going to extend that vacation a few more days. But if you need me on the defense subcommittee, I'm available. Is there anything on the docket?"

There was a pause while she checked. "Nothing right now, but I'll let you know."

"Great. And is Simpson really pissed off at me? I mean, more than normal? Like does he have an actual reason I should be aware of?"

She let out a small chuckle. "No, just his usual grumpiness. I think his wife is holding out on him again. That boy really needs to get laid on a regular basis or he just makes everyone's life hell."

"Sounds like *need to know* information, and I did *not* need to know that."

Shelley laughed, and it was a good sound to hear. Piper trusted her to give a little heads up—or insist that Piper come into the office—if anything serious was going down. Which, if Simpson had any clue what she had been up to, would constitute a major crisis.

"All right," Piper said, "let me know if anything comes up. I'll be taking the next few days for some personal business. Hope to wrap it up really soon. Can't wait to get back in the field."

"You got it." The line clicked off.

Piper strode down the hallway, making the last few turns to reach Michael's office, which was adjacent to Krepky's larger, official Senate office. She didn't bother knocking, just opened the door, right on time. Michael sat at his desk, peering at something on his screen, but he looked up when she closed the door behind her.

A smile lit his face. He was young—probably no more than 30—and not terribly unattractive, but he had a smarmy way about him. His smiles were the kind that were calculated to either win votes for his boss or threaten people into backing him. Everything served a purpose in his grander scheme.

"Piper!" he effused, rising from his chair. "Can't tell you how glad I am to see you."

"I'm sure you could tell me," Piper said in a voice that invited the flirtation she knew he enjoyed. "But I don't really have time for flattery right now. This is just a quickie visit, Michael."

He gave her an exaggerated pout as he rounded the desk, then strode forward for one of his patented, far-too-familiar hugs, the kind he gave all the pretty assistants and interns. She allowed it, but couldn't help comparing it to Jace's quick embrace: where Michael left her feeling chilled, Jace had set every part of her on fire.

She shoved that thought out of her mind. *Focus, Piper.*

When Michael released her, she said, "Look, I know you're busy, so I won't waste any of your time."

He gave her a flirtatious smile. "Time with you is never a waste, Piper Wilding. Still waiting to find out if you live up to your last name."

So… that's how it was going to be. Piper held in her sigh. "Not sure I have time for that today, Michael." She hadn't slept with him—yet—but that had always been dangled as a possibility. And before today, she probably would have used this opportunity to initiate Michael into her list of "not-definitively-bad" guys who she slept with to score information necessary to her job. She drew the line at sleeping with the definitively bad guys, as a general rule, unless necessary… but in her line of business there were often a lot of gray areas. And an orgasm was an orgasm. Didn't really matter who it was with. Until… until Jace River cruised into her life and held out the promise of more. *A whole lot more.* And suddenly the Michael's of the world got shoved off the "maybe" list onto the "no way in hell" list.

Which made the idea of sleeping with him now give her the creeps.

Michael leaned forward and swept a lock of her long, black hair over her shoulder, a touch as calculated as it was shudder-worthy. "Oh, come on, Piper. You've been teasing me so long, I'm not sure I can withstand a rejection at this point."

She forced a flirtatious smile onto her face and leaned into him, fussing with his collar and giving him a long, hot look straight in the eyes. "I'm not saying *never*… I'm just saying I don't have time to do it properly right now."

He took that as a license to pull her closer, sliding his hands around her waist and yanking her body up against his. His erection poked her stomach, and she had to force herself to keep the smile and not actually throw up in his face.

It was so obvious that Jace River had *already* ruined her—*bad*—for anyone else. And she hadn't even slept with him. *Damn him.*

"I hear shifter women are extraordinarily hot and dirty in bed." Michael leered and came close to kissing her, but held back. "How about a taste as a little down payment?" Then he kissed her, forcing his tongue into her mouth and digging around like he was searching for some kind of buried treasure.

*God.* Noah had better survive whatever trouble he was in, so she could beat the shit out of him for putting her through this. She made a mental note to replay all the gory details for him once he was safe again. Thinking about that got her through the kiss. When it was over, Michael pulled back and gave her a little space. *Thank God.*

"Too bad I can't stay and play." Piper pulled back a little farther. "But like I said, not much time today. Just need to know something."

Michael was all smiles and erection still pressing into her side "What can I help you with, hot little Piper?"

She played with his collar again. "I was wondering if there was some kind of new program the Senator was looking to start. Something having to do with shifters."

"Why do you ask that?" He frowned a little.

"Some rumors I heard. About shifters in special programs, possibly in the military." There, she said it. She couldn't get too close to the truth without having him clam up tight.

*"That,* my hot shifter girl, is classified information. I'd need a lot more inducement to give you all the details of a program involving shifters."

Which only confirmed the existence of one.

Piper leaned close again and gave him a soft kiss that lingered—more erotic and less *slobbering dog,* the way he'd kissed her. It was remarkably difficult to pull off—the only way she got through it was by closing her eyes and imagining Jace was on the receiving end.

When she stopped, Michael was breathing hard. *"Damn.* I am so going to enjoy fucking you."

She had to repress the shudder. "Consider that an advance for a little more information about this program involving shifters. I promise to make it up to you later."

He wet his lips, hesitated, and finally said, "Let's just say the Senator has big plans for shifters. He'll be making a public announcement soon, anyway, so I guess there's not much harm in telling you what's coming."

She waited.

"You know the Senator's long been interested in the way that the government can use the resources that shifters possess. He's recently become more concerned about those who aren't in our military programs or government programs, such as yourself. He's looking at proposing a new registration system."

She frowned. "Registration? You mean like what we already do with the police?" Any shifter—including her, especially those in the military or government service already, but really anyone who had been identified as a shifter—had to provide DNA samples to the police in both their shifter and human forms. They basically assumed that shifters were criminals just waiting to commit a crime, and the government wanted to have them on file, just in case.

"No, that's not what I mean." His hold on her got a little tighter. "Piper, he's going to start advocating for registration of the general public. You know I have a soft spot for shifters…" He gave her a squeeze. "But the Senator is more concerned about the danger your kind might present."

She pulled back. "Danger? There are shifters serving in the military. And in the government. We're *part of* the

US government. How can he think we're a danger?"

Michael shrugged, but he loosened his hold and moved back to the other side of the desk. "It's just politics, Piper. You understand."

She understood, all too well. And she was about to burn a bridge the Senator's office if she didn't get her ass out of there—immediately. "I understand," she said thickly.

She turned and strode towards Michael's office door.

"Send me a text when you get a little free time," Michael called after her. "I can't wait to cash in that advance."

She ignored him and left before she said something she would regret.

# Chapter 9

Jace had been pacing the same dozen feet in front of the window in the great room of the safehouse for the last hour, hoping Piper would just show up. He didn't know where she had gone exactly, but he suspected she was at Senator Krepky's office in the capitol... which could only mean she was getting in trouble again. He'd utterly failed to stop her from running off, and he'd been kicking himself every minute since. Like an idiot, he hadn't even gotten her phone number. He literally let her run off with no way to contact her. He was cursing himself pretty spectacularly about that, too.

His brothers and the rest of the wolves who'd gone on the mission had returned to the safehouse as well, each now off on some task to try to unravel this mystery. Piper's brother, Daniel, had gone back to the Joint Base, clearly unconvinced that anything at all was happening. But Jace and the rest of them knew—the makeshift military hospital they had discovered was just the kind of setup Agent Smith would use to experiment on shifters. Jace had no doubt there were more shifters still under his control, and he trusted Piper's instincts on this—Noah was one of them.

His brother Jared pounded down the stairs.

Jace stopped his pacing. "Any news?"

Jared had a fistful of papers in one hand and tablet in the other. He slowed his rush into the room and examined Jace for a moment. "Nothing about Piper. But I might have a trace on Agent Smith."

Jaxson, who had been talking in the kitchen with Olivia, must've heard because the two of them quickly strolled into the room. "What do you have?" he asked.

"He's definitely still in the Seattle Metro area," said Jared. "I've got three separate pings on him: a convenience store, a McDonald's, and an ATM. All on the south side of Seattle."

"So he's a resident," Jace said. "Any way to nail down his identity? What about the ATM? Can we pull bank records and tie him to an account?"

Jared grimaced. "Yeah, but you're not gonna believe this. It's registered to a John Smith."

Jace groaned. "So this is deep, deep cover for him."

"And probably going on for some time," Jaxson added.

"I'll see if I can nail down some patterns of activity. Maybe, if we get lucky, we can intercept Agent Smith on the way to the dry cleaners."

Jace snorted. "Somehow I don't think our luck is that good." He sighed.

Jaxson shrugged. "I still think we should go to the witches."

Olivia nodded—she had been standing quietly behind him, listening to the conversation. "I'm sure my aunt Gwen and her coven could do a better job with a seeking spell than I did. But I would have to go down to the coven."

"I don't want to put Piper through that again." Jace folded his arms across his chest. "What did you see during the spell that freaked her out so badly?"

Olivia pursed her lips, hesitated, then said, "It's not my place to tell you, Jace. But I agree—it would not be good to put her through that again."

A crunch of tires on the gravel road outside the safehouse drew everyone's attention to the window. The sun was setting, and it was nearly dark as a small black sedan pulled up. Piper jumped out and hurried to the front door. Jace unlocked his arms and ran to open the door before she got there.

"Piper," he said as she arrived. "Are you all right—"

He cut off as she rushed up to him—she seemed like she was going to throw her arms around him, but then pulled back at the last second.

Instead, she just gripped his arm. "Jace." She was breathless. "This is bad. Really bad."

Jace frowned. "Whatever it is, we'll handle it. *Together.*" He tugged her inside and closed the door. Then he slipped his hand into hers—he was a little surprised she didn't object, but she had a thoroughly freaked-out look on her face, and he didn't like that one bit. He ushered her into the great room where his brothers and Olivia were watching them with quiet, intense expressions.

Jace gestured to them. "We've been working on

another way to find Noah, as well as Agent Smith." He pulled her closer with their clasped hands. "What did you find the Senator's office?"

She scanned the faces in the room, hesitating—once again, she seemed to be calculating who she could trust and who she couldn't.

She shook her head and blurted out, "Senator Krepky is planning on calling for registration for all shifters."

"Registration?" Jaxson frowned. "You mean the kind where we have to come in and register openly as shifters?"

"But…" Olivia looked vaguely horrified. "There's a reason why you guys keep it secret, right?"

"The reason being that most people fear and hate us? Yes." Jared's voice was cold and harsh. But it was the truth.

"But that would ruin Riverwise," Olivia said, the horror becoming more plain. "And every other shifter business. How can he even propose doing that? What about civil rights? What about—"

"Krepky doesn't give a shit about any of that." Piper cut her off, but not in a mean way—more like she was just trying to get to the point. "It's all about politics for him. He's just playing off the fears of the people. I don't even know if he would have the votes to put something like that through, or if it would sustain in the courts, but he's going to do it. And when he does…" Her lovely face paled.

"And when he does, the pressure will be on," Jace finished for her. "Shifters will be outed anyway. Friends, neighbors, anyone… a proposal like that would just fan their fears. It could endanger everything in the shifter community." *Shit.* This was even worse than he thought. He turned back to Piper. "Did you find anything more about the military shifters who are missing?"

Her face reddened. On any other woman, he would take it as a blush, but on Piper, he didn't know what to make of it. "I can't use my normal methods to get that kind of information." Her teeth were grinding, and she was forcing the words through them. "I'm going to have to hack into the Senator's files from the outside or break into his office—basically, steal them outright instead of bribing for them. But I'm sure the information is there. I'm sure he's doing *something.* His assistant all but acknowledged the existence of a secret program—he just wouldn't give me the details. Without a price. One I'm not really willing to pay."

Jace's wolf surged and roiled under his skin—he could

too easily guess what kind of price a man would exact from a gorgeous woman like Piper, and the idea of another man touching her nearly brought his wolf to the surface in a fit of jealousy mixed with a violent need to protect her from that kind of predation. He was glad she had said no to whatever was asked, but he didn't like the alternative, either—hacking into a Senator's files would likely land her in jail.

Jace squeezed her hand. "You're not doing any of that—"

She yanked her hand from his, and her face darkened further. "You don't get to tell me what to do, Jace River—"

Before she could finish, a subtle beep came from her pocket, and she cut herself off midsentence. The frown on her face was equal parts concern and surprise. She fished her phone out of her pocket, and her father's face loomed large, looking angry and spiteful.

Piper flashed a look to Jace, and he hated the fear in her eyes. "You have to take it," he said. "But we're right here. It's going to be okay."

She shook her head rapidly, as if she hardly was controlling the motion, and it was born of a deep, primal fear. She seemed to force herself to tap the phone to accept the call. The Colonel's face came to life—a Facetime call.

"You just can't leave things alone, can you?" The Colonel demanded in a harsh voice, no preamble whatsoever.

"Nice to see you too, Father." Piper's voice was strong and defiant, but Jace could see the widening of her eyes. And he suspected the Colonel could too. That was probably why he was Facetiming—so he could use his commanding presence to intimidate her. Just one more thing to loath about the man.

Jared, Jaxson, and Olivia held stark still, listening in as well.

"I hear you've been sneaking around again," the Colonel said sneer. "I don't know what you think you're going to accomplish with this, Piper, but you're out of your depth."

Piper scowled at him. "Noah is your *son*. I know that doesn't mean anything to you, but—"

The Colonel snarled into the phone. "I don't need to be lectured by a bastard about how to run my family! I've had no use for you since the day you were born. Your mother would still be around if it weren't for you, so don't give me any shit about *family*. All you've ever done is ruin it."

Jace's wolf surged again. His mouth hung open, aghast, then snapped shut in fury. Who the fuck did this guy think he was? How could he talk to his own daughter that way? Jace stumbled forward and practically grabbed the phone out of Piper's hand—he wanted to give that guy a piece of his mind—but Piper elbowed him out of the way and huddled over the phone, shoulders bowed, as if she could hide this conversation from the prying eyes in the room.

"You're not exactly winning Father of the Year Award, *Daddy.*" Her voice was harsh, but Jace could see the shaking of her shoulders. "Just tell me where Noah is and what you're doing to him. I know you're involved in this somehow—"

Her father snorted, an ugly sound. "That information is so far above your pay grade, you wouldn't even understand it if I told you." The menacing look he gave her seemed to reach across the phone line and run a shiver through her body. "But let me be very clear, Piper—if you keep looking for Noah, you won't be missing just *one* brother."

*"What?"* Her shoulders dropped, and her face paled. "What have you done to Daniel?"

Her father sneered. "He's already disappointed me once today: he was weak and unprepared to deal with *you*. He didn't understand what a dangerous and disturbed thing you are. But if you keep poking around, Piper, your brother will pay for it and in more ways than just a pay cut and some furlough time. Whatever happens to Daniel will be on your head."

Piper's mouth dropped open. "How can you… how can you just…?" She seemed to be gasping for air.

"This is your only warning." Her father's face disappeared, the phone switching to black as the call cut off.

Piper's hand shook, making the phone quiver, then slowly sunk to her side. "He's a monster." Her voice was a whisper, not really speaking to any of them.

Jace lurched forward and grabbed her by the shoulders to spin her around and hold her tight… but it was like holding onto a wildcat. She turned, claws out and slashing across his shirt before he even realized what was happening. Blood spread across the white linen, but the slicing pain was nothing compared to watching her flail out of his grasp, growling and crying and sobbing all at once.

"Piper… Piper, stop it," he stammered.

She pointed an accusing finger at him. "You don't know him! He'll do it! He'll take both of them…" Her shaking hand fell back to her side, defeated.

Jace edged closer to her, hands out, not moving so fast this time. "Let me help you." He gestured to Olivia. "The coven can do another seeking spell—"

Piper's eyes widened, and if it was possible, her face went even more pale. Ghostly. "I'm not doing that again."

Olivia stepped forward. "You don't need to. The memory is vivid enough in my own mind now—with my Aunt Gwen's help, we could do the seeking spell without you. The only thing is… we would have to do it with the whole coven. Aunt Gwen says she can draw more magical energy from inside the Damon Design office, with all the witches there at once, even if they're not all involved in the spell."

Jace turned back to Piper. "See? We can do this. We'll find him."

Piper was shaking her head in a small quivering motion.

Jaxson took Olivia's hand in his. "We'll do what we can, but it'll probably have to wait until morning. I'm pretty sure Damon Design is closed for the day."

*"The morning?"* Piper gasped, her voice rising again. "I can't wait until then! You heard him—he's going to pull Daniel into the same secret program that has taken Noah. He'll do it no matter what I say, no matter what I do, just to spite me. I have to move *now!"* She turned to storm towards the door.

Jace lunged after her, catching her by the elbow. "Wait! My brothers will call Daniel and warn him."

Piper whirled on him, but this time her claws stayed sheathed. "He won't believe you!"

"Jaxson will convince him." Jace motioned subtly to the others in the room, who were quickly getting the hint and filing out to the kitchen. He kept his voice calm, in spite of the rising panic of his wolf pushing to get out. "We have to give Olivia time to do this right. Just until the morning. Then we'll know if the coven can find him or not."

She was back to shaking her head again. "I have to get back to the Senator's office… I have to find out where they're keeping Noah before it's too late…" There was a dazed look in her eyes, crazy and in pain, and it tore through Jace to see it.

"It's too dangerous, Piper."

"You can't stop me!"

Jace sighed. "No, I can't stop you. But, please, just give me a couple minutes. Give me a chance. We can talk in private." He tilted his head toward the stairs and prayed she would just grant him this one thing. He just needed to get her away from the door and cooled down, so he could figure out how to keep her from running off again. Because he had a sick, sick feeling in his stomach that if he didn't stop her this time, she would be the next one to disappear.

And he would lose her forever.

To his immeasurable relief, she gave him one, small nod. "Five minutes," she said, thickly, her eyes glazed.

"Five minutes," he agreed, holding back the smile that wanted to burst forth.

She dully walked up the steps, and he followed close behind. She was in pain—he could tell by each heavy step—and he would give anything to erase that.

# CHAPTER 10

Piper's feet seemed to catch on every small bump in the polished wood floor of the safehouse hallway. Jace led her to one of the many, identical rooms—once she was inside, she realized it must be his bedroom. The sheets on the bed were rumpled, as if he had just gotten out of it... or perhaps never made it. Clothes were strewn haphazardly around the room.

Jace closed the door behind them.

Piper turned to face him, the dull weight of the Colonel's words and threats still pulling her down like a boulder around her neck. "You have five minutes, Jace River." She was so tired. She needed to catch her breath and clear her head, before she would have any chance pulling off this idea of infiltrating the Senator's office.

Jace closed the distance between them and took her hand. "I know your father pisses you off, but fuck that guy. Don't let your anger at him drive you into doing something dangerous."

"I do dangerous things all the time." Even she could hear the dullness in her voice.

He gave a small smile. "I know. But you're smart about it. When you're out in the field, you don't let anyone run your life. You don't let some asshole with a bunch of military awards tell you what to do. Besides, the Colonel doesn't know what the hell he's talking about."

She closed her eyes briefly, then opened them and looked straight up into the Jace's dark, caring eyes. "He *does* know what he's talking about, at least when it comes to me."

"He doesn't know anything about you." Jace's face darkened. "That couldn't be more clear from the way he treats you."

Piper turned away from him, folded her arms, and faced the door. Jace didn't know about her past. Staring at the door, she said, "You've got three minutes, Jace River."

Jace loomed at her back without touching her. "The Piper I know faces down military MPs and sneaks into a house full of shifters. What did you see during Olivia's spell that scared you so badly? Did he... did your father *do* something to you when you were a kid?"

"He didn't do anything to me." She unlocked her arms and let them hang by her side. "He hated me before I was even born." She turned to face him. The confusion on his face was mixed with a kind of sadness—a concern she'd never seen before, not directed at *her,* anyway. It worked a kind of magic inside her, prying loose the truth and forcing it up to her lips.

"He called me a bastard." She huffed a small, mirthless laugh. "And it's true. I'm not really his daughter. The Colonel fought and killed my biological father. He wanted my mother for his own, but she was already mated to another man. It wasn't until after he shattered the mating bond by killing my biological father, that the Colonel discovered my mother was already pregnant. Even she didn't know she had a pup growing inside her. *Me.* The Colonel wanted her to abort me. He literally wished I had never been born. My mother refused, but ever since I came into the world, he's resented me. After that, he wanted a new pup, a *real* progeny, so he forced himself upon my mother for years, trying to impregnate her. She secretly took birth-control pills to stop it, but when she was finally discovered, the Colonel threw them all away and finally got what he wanted: *Daniel.* The Colonel always treated me like I was the kid who didn't exist. But that wasn't the worst of it."

Jace's horrified expression was working its way into her heart, loosening her tongue even further, spilling out things she had never told anyone—not anyone who didn't already know, like Noah.

"What the hell… what kind of alpha does *that?*" Jace was aghast, and she was sure that in the perfect world of the River brothers, with a loving family and mates who adored them, this kind of thing must seem… impossible.

"He was the kind who abused everyone… including my mother. I don't think he actually hit her—although I don't know what happened behind their closed bedroom door. I think the mating bond, perhaps, protected her a little. At least enough so that he didn't actually kill her. But he made her so miserable, she decided to take care of that herself."

She had to stop talking because her throat was closing

up too much.

Jace moved even closer. Her back was up against the door—the door she had been ready to charge out of just a moment ago—and he was so close, they could almost touch.

"Piper, I'm so sorry." His voice was a gentle whisper that knocked loose the words again.

"The mating bond killed her. That, and having a bastard child with a mate who didn't want me. So, you see, I really did ruin everything."

*"Piper.* No—"

"No, it's true." She put both hands on his chest and pushed him slightly away, unable to deal with the fact that he was so close and so caring and so concerned with those dark, gorgeous eyes. "I long ago swore off mating. I saw what it did to my mother. And I was worthless, good for nothing to my father... except whatever he could sell me for as mate for some other asshole alpha he knew." Tears were coming up unbidden to her eyes. "I was never good for anything but a strategic alliance. It was the only thing I could take from him. So I did—I left. I vowed never to mate. And I've been running my life my own way ever since. And now he's ruining my brothers' lives with some other damn scheme of his that

I'm sure increases his power or prestige or something. And I'm not going to let him do it! I'm not to let him take the one thing that matters to me in this world, the only person who's ever given a damn about me—Noah was there when Mom died. He knows the truth about how our father is, what he's really like."

She was trembling so hard and backed up so much against the door, it felt like all her insides were going to spill out. The look on Jace's face—pitying and horrified—just twisted her stomach more. He reached for her cheek. She tipped her head back, but there was nowhere to go. He held her with a gentle touch that just wrenched the tears from her eyes and made them spill down her face.

"Your father is wrong. About everything, but especially about you." His words, soft and close, made her tremble. "No true alpha does something like that. No decent man treats a daughter that way. I don't give a fuck if you're his biological daughter or not. You were born of his mate, the woman he was supposed to treasure and care for and love above all things. If *I* had a daughter, you can be sure I would treasure her like the moon and the stars. Like the love I would have for her mother, my mate. You don't treat a *dog* the way your father has treated you, much less a beautiful woman. A gorgeous, smart, incredible woman. He's wrong about everything… and I'm not going to let him manipulate you into doing something that will only get you hurt."

She wrenched her face out of his hold and turned around to face the door again. She slammed her palm against it once, twice, three times, and let out a growl. Why did Jace have to be such a good man? The kind she could never have. Why did he have to say those words to her? Didn't he know her anger was the only thing that kept her going?

She grabbed the doorknob and yanked on it, but his hands against the door held it closed. "Let me out of here!" she screamed as she pounded her fist against the wood.

"Piper." His voice was soft, but with an underlying command tone that rippled through her like a shiver. "Turn around."

She closed her eyes and let her head fall against the door. Then she turned around, still trapped in the cage of his arms on either side of her, his palms pressed against the door. She looked up into his dark eyes, and they didn't just hold concern anymore. They were blazing at her with a dark heat that lit fires all over her body.

"You're not going to leave," he said, soft and powerful. "You're going to stay here and do exactly what I tell you."

A shiver worked its way up her body, coursing heat and lust through her. Her wolf responded to his alpha tone, whimpering for him. The woman in her wanted to protest. The angry girl in her wanted to slam her fists against his chest. But Jace was a better man than any man she'd ever known, and he was looking at her like he *wanted* her. Not just for sex. Not the way sleazy Michael wanted to fuck her. Jace's heated, possessive, yet soft-and-caring look said he wanted her in *every* way—to protect, to keep safe, and to ravish against the door of his bedroom.

She couldn't force herself to say no.

He leaned in close, his commanding voice strong and soft. "You're not as wild as you act… not as crazy as you pretend. You're smart and strong and you don't need to let that asshole control you anymore. Because you're not alone. You don't have to do any of this on your own. Everyone should have someone at their back, and I'm going to be that for you, Piper. I will *be there* for you, through all of this. To the end."

His words were an earthquake, shaking her to her

core. A small part of her dared to believe him, and that sent even larger shockwaves through her body.

He leaned even closer. "Now kiss me, dammit."

It was a command, one she didn't even want to think of disobeying. She leaned forward, closing the small distance left between them, and very tentatively pressed her lips to his. She was trembling so hard, her lips barely brushed against him, but the heat of his lips touching hers raced sparks throughout her body.

"No," he whispered, his voice husky, "Not like that." He slid one of his hands away from the door and threaded his fingers through her hair, grabbing a fistful and tilting her head back, lips opening up to him. "Like this."

Then he crashed his lips into hers, devouring her. His body slammed hers against the door, his leg already between hers, forcing them open. His urgent, powerful kiss and the grip on her hair demanded that she open her mouth to him, not that she even thought of hesitating. His tongue plundered her mouth, demanding that she yield to him even more. Heat flushed hard and fast to her panties, soaking them as his hand found her breast, grabbing and squeezing it and making her moan. The sound echoed a rumbling deep in his chest. Only then did she notice his erection, powerful and rock-hard against her stomach, reminding her of what she first glimpsed on his kitchen floor... and what she'd fantasized about having fill her ever since.

Jace finally broke the kiss, just for a moment, but her hands were already on his shoulders, pulling him back. He growled and pulled her head farther to the side, devouring her neck in a serious of hot, wet kisses that practically made her come with their intensity. He feasted on her, working his way up to her ear, then hoarsely whispered, "Piper, I need to be inside you."

Her answer was to let her hand fall to the mountain of cock pressing between them and giving him one hard stroke. She wanted all of him. Inside her. *Now.*

He groaned a feral, wolfish growl that raised every hair on her body—with excitement and lust—and her wolf was already in the submission position, ready to give everything to him.

She gasped with that realization. *No! Not submission.* No, she couldn't... but as Jace's mouth greedily devoured hers again, and his hand shoved down her pants to find the sopping wet core between her legs, she knew he wasn't asking that. He wanted to fill her with his cock and his love... not his magic. Not the bite that would forever bind her to him.

He wanted her love and her body... and *those* she could give him. In fact, she had never wanted to give them to a man so badly in her life.

She tried to shove down his jeans but got nowhere. Jace pulled back enough to unbutton and work loose his pants, springing his cock free. It was even larger than she seen tenting out his sleep pants before, and her mouth watered. She wanted to suck him, make him come in her mouth, have him in a dozen different ways. She wanted to pray at the altar of that gorgeous piece of man flesh and the amazing man who owned it, but before she could get her hands on it, he was grabbing her blouse and ripping it apart. Buttons flew, and he practically tore her bra from her body. She was bare up top now, and his hooded eyes said he wanted to spend time there, but she couldn't wait. She tugged at her own pants, but her hands were still a shaking mess. He shoved them aside and dropped to one knee, plastering hot, wet kisses on her belly as he undid her pants and slid them down her hips. As soon as her sex was exposed, his tongue found it. She gasped with the sudden electric spark of pleasure as he darted in, sweeping across her nub. She grabbed his head, pulling him closer.

"Oh, God, Jace. Fuck." She was panting and barely able to form coherent words.

His hands were still working her panties off her body as his tongue worked her soaking wet core. "Oh, yes, my love. We're going to do that. But first, I'm going to enjoy myself a little." As soon as her panties were free, he thrust two fingers inside her, pumping her as his tongue flicked across her nub.

"Jace!" She clutched at him, but she was racing to orgasm, and it caught her like a wave that swept her off her feet, throbbing and pulsing all over her body. "Oh God. Oh God." She kept saying it over and over, with every thrust of his fingers and every convulsion of pleasure. She'd barely crested the top when he pulled out and stood, his hands on her hips, holding her steady—which was good because her knees were so weak they could barely hold her up against the door.

The grin on Jace's face was all wolf. "Tell me you want me," he commanded.

"I want you." Oh God, how she wanted him inside her.

He gripped her hips, hoisting her up and pressing her against the wall. His enormous cock nudged against her entrance. She could barely catch her breath, and the anticipation was killing her… but he only teased her with it, not giving her what she desperately wanted.

His breathing was just as ragged as hers. He leaned in to whisper, "Tell me you're not going to run away."

"I'm not running away." Wasn't that obvious? Although she probably would have said anything at that point, just to have him take her, hard, up against the door.

He thrust inside her, and she gasped—he had to be the largest man she'd ever had. He stretched and filled her in a way that made her whimper and grab hold of him. But he remained still, sheathed inside her, unmoving.

"Goddamit, Jace, what do I have to *say?*" she begged.

She could feel the heat of his smirk on her, but she didn't care—all she wanted was for him to *move*. To make love to her. To own her body against the door like it belonged to him.

He moved ever-so-slightly, and it coursed pleasure through her, but then he stopped again. "Tell me you're going to stay and let me love you," he whispered, and this time it was soft, less demanding, more questioning.

Her heart cracked wide open. She sobbed, then the words spilled out. "I'll stay."

"And let me love you." His words were a tremor that shattered her again.

"Please love me." The words came out as sobs, but then he moved inside her, thrusting hard, and her sobs turned into shrieks of pleasure. He pumped into her, furiously, groaning his own pleasure, taking her hard, building on the shockwaves already coursing through her body, taking her higher. She'd never experienced anything like this—this emotional wrenching, this surge of pleasure and love, all wrapped into one writhing mess of bodies slick with heat. She clung to him, riding him like the hurricane he was, sweeping into her life and changing everything... changing *her*... breaking her down, turning her inside out, and putting her back together again.

A tightness coiled deep inside her, more than pleasure, building to an ecstasy that felt like it would change everything. "Oh, God, Jace, I'm going to come." Her words were back to being sobs.

He ground into her even harder, thrusting and angling just right. "Come for me, baby." His voice was ragged, looser than before. It made her heart lurch. There was something wrong. Something terribly wrong with that sound... but his groans, and his mouth clamping on her neck, with the hard points of his fangs sheathed by his lips, held back, not claiming her but still teasing her with their sharpness… it pushed her right over the edge.

She screamed his name and came so hard she bucked them both away from the door again and again as he held her tight.

He growled, and she thought he had reached his release, too… but instead, he suddenly wrenched away from her and staggered back, leaving her panting and hollow against the door. His erection stood tall in the waning sunlight spilling through his window, and his fangs were bared, claws out, with a wild look in his eyes.

"Get out!" he yelled.

His words sliced through her heart.

Then he turned his back on her.

# CHAPTER 11

*Holy fuck, what was he doing?*

Jace struggled with his beast, wrestled with it, cursed and shouted and summoned every ounce of will he had to shove it back deep inside him. He watched as his claws receded, felt his fangs tuck back into his mouth, and his heaving breath mixed with sighs of relief. What was he thinking? That he could take Piper like that, the way he wanted to—the way his *wolf* wanted to—and not risk his beast bursting forth? He knew she needed to hear those words, to feel his body, to know what he felt for her was more than just lust… but he'd gotten too lost in it.

And almost lost control.

Her words from before haunted him—*I ruin everything.* He wanted to kill the man who told this little girl she didn't matter in the world. Because she was starting to be *everything* to him—someone who needed him; someone he could care for; someone he could rescue to make up for all the lives he had destroyed. And he'd almost let his wolf loose on her. A shudder ran through him, but his beast was quiet again, even though his hard-on was still raging.

He turned back to Piper. She was naked and horrified, laid bare physically and emotionally against his door. Her expression speared through him. She had to wonder, had to *know*, there was something terribly wrong with him, but he couldn't let her go for one second more thinking it had anything to do with *her*—because he could see it all over her face.

He'd told her to get out.

*Fuck.*

He lumbered back toward her. "Piper, I'm sorry."

"I can… I can… leave now…" She was hysterical,

looking everywhere in the room but at him. "I'll just… get my clothes…" She bent to pick up the scraps he'd torn from her body.

God, he had messed this up so badly. His body was still coursing heat from their lovemaking, and his hard-on stuck out from his body like an awkward additional limb, but he didn't let any of that stop him from pulling her up from where she crouched on the floor and gathering her into his arms. She was trembling again. Because of him. And not in a good way.

"You're not going anywhere," he said, his voice less ragged, now that his beast was under control. "Come with me to the bed."

She was blinking and shaking. "I don't… I don't understand."

"I know. Let me explain," he said softly, slipping his hands down her body. Damn, she was so soft and delicious… his hard-on wasn't going anywhere at this rate. But he eased her toward the bed with him, holding her around the waist because her legs didn't seem so steady. When they reached it, he drew her down into his lap as he sat on the edge. His erection made its presence known, but he ignored that, pushing a wild lock of her gorgeous black hair behind her ear. She was so goddamn beautiful—and so open and vulnerable to him right now. He felt like he was holding a kitten. A very *sexy* kitten… but a fragile, beautiful thing, nonetheless.

"I have a secret to tell you." His chest clenched because she might run from him. She might decide he was too dangerous to be around or just plain evil. But he obviously couldn't risk making love to her—his beast was too easily drawn to the surface by her—and she deserved to know why.

Her dark eyes were wide, her body still flushed from their lovemaking. Her nipples were tight, and he couldn't help running his hands up the gentle curve of her waist to lightly trace the flesh hardened with pleasure. He could spend the rest of the night just playing with her gorgeous breasts.

"I think I've already figured out that you like my breasts," she said with a small smile.

It made him laugh and broke his heart at the same time. "You have no idea how much I like your breasts," he said, his voice suddenly going husky again. His cock twitched… and that really wasn't where this needed to go. "Maybe I'll show you later. But first, there's something you need to know about me: I can't shift."

The smile dropped from her face. "But I saw you…"

Realization dawned on her face. "You said before that you choose *not* to shift. Why?" She was open and curious now. Unafraid.

For the moment.

"Because I can't control my beast." He said it quietly, but he could count the heartbeats between his words and her response.

A frown slowly drew down her face. "What do you mean?"

"I mean that, when I shift, I turn into a wild animal, not a man in wolf clothing."

To her credit, she didn't immediately pull away in horror. In fact, she just looked perplexed. "I've never heard of anything like that."

"It's pretty rare." He cleared his throat. He was unusual in more ways than that. "In fact, I'm the only one I know with this… affliction. But it means that I can't risk shifting, not when anyone else is around, at least."

"But you're still a wolf, right?" Her voice was light, like she was still trying to puzzle out what he was saying.

He should just come out and tell her all of it. "Yes and no. My wolf is… large. Massive really. Twice the size of any normal wolf. And crazy strong. Plus he's always been… well, a bit on the wild side." He smiled a little and squeezed her waist, teasing her about her name.

She shook her head. "Maybe you're not as wild as you pretend."

That dropped the humor from his face. "My wolf has always been hard to control. And that was before…" He sucked in a breath, then just forced the words out. "When I was deployed, I lost control of my wolf, and a lot of people died because of it."

She was frowning again, but not pulling away. "What happened?"

He gritted his teeth, but there was no holding back now. "My troop was on patrol. Afghanistan. We were going to check on a remote village that had some reports of insurgent activity. When we were almost there, our Jeep must have hit an IED or something—all I remember was being thrown in the air and shifting on the way down. After that… it's a blur. I can only remember bits and pieces. The burning village. The people…" His voice hitched, and he had to choke back the horror and guilt welling up. "Later, when I woke up in a hospital, they told me—everyone in the Jeep died. The entire village had been wiped out. They were either blown up by the IED or torn to pieces by some kind of wild animal."

Her eyes went wide. "You think it was your wolf?"

"It *was* my wolf, Piper." He sighed. He could still see his patrol's faces, just before everything went to hell—Owen, Wyatt, Anthony. He was the only one who came back. He hadn't been able to face their families either, just slunk off to join Jaxson and Jared at Riverwise. "I can't remember it all, just snatches of what happened that come back to me in my dreams. My nightmares. But I was there—*in the village*—or rather, my wolf was. I can smell the burning flesh. I can see the fear in their eyes—" He had to stop and look away from her beautiful, concerned face. He couldn't change what had happened, and he would forever regret losing control, but the only thing that mattered now was making damn sure it never happened again. He cleared his throat and looked back to her. "The tribunal investigating the incident ruled it technically as an "accident." But they left the cause as "unknown attack by a wild animal." They let me leave with an honorable discharge. But it's a lie—I know it, and they know it." He gently touched his fingertips to her cheek. "It means I can't *ever* shift again. I can't submit to my alpha, I can't take a mate… I can't ever be anything more than a man. And some days, I feel lucky to even have that chance."

A roil of emotions churned across Piper's face, and he half expected her to bolt. Instead, she moved slightly in his lap, her beautiful soft skin sliding against his, and gripped his cheeks with both of her small hands.

She gave him a fierce look. "You are a *good* man."

He closed his eyes briefly. "Piper—"

"Shut up. I'm talking."

His mouth hung open for a second, then he smirked. "Yes, Ma'am."

But she didn't say anything else—she just gripped his cheeks harder and kissed him. It was intense and fast and the taste of her, the *feel* of her grinding against him, sitting naked in his lap, made his cock spring to attention. By the time she pulled back, he was breathing hard again.

"I like the way you talk," he said, the smirk still playing on his face.

"Now you listen to me," she demanded, eyes blazing. "You are one of the bravest, most selfless, most honorable men I've ever met. And there's no way in hell you took out a village of innocent civilians. I don't care what form you were in."

His shoulders dropped. "Piper, please—"

"I'm still talking." She mock glared at him, and he couldn't help it—it wrenched another smile out of him.

"If you don't want to shift, *fine*. If you want to believe your beast is something different than *you,* fine. But I want you to know that *I* know the truth about you, Jace River. And the truth is, you're good and decent, through to the core, like no one I've ever known. You're the kind of man I'd trust with my life… the kind I'd trust with my heart. And there are literally no others in that category."

She held his gaze. It took a long moment for him to realize what she said, and more importantly: *she wasn't running away.* Then she leaned in and kissed him again, slower this time, less intense but more erotic, like her tongue wanted to take its sweet time exploring his mouth. He couldn't believe she was still here, still kissing him, still naked in his lap, when she knew—she *knew*—everything that he was. He held her tight and kissed her back. But when she reached down to stroke his raging hard-on, he caught her wrist and pulled it away.

"I can't." His voice was heavy with lust. God, how he wanted her to keep going. "It's not safe. My beast almost broke loose before—"

"You're not going to hurt me." The confidence in her voice was… insane. Did she not hear all the things he just explained?

"I mean it, Piper."

"Shut up. I'm talking again." But she wasn't—she was sliding off his lap to kneel between his legs on the floor in front of him.

"Piper, what are you—" But he didn't have to ask, because she gripped his cock and slid her hot little mouth over it. *"Fuck."* The feel as she took him deep in her throat, the insanely erotic sight of her lips sliding over him, her tight fist stroking the length that she couldn't take in... all of it made his eyes roll back in his head. He gripped her hair in his fist to stop her, but she just sucked harder and wrenched a moan out of him. He ended up guiding her head as it bobbed in his lap, and he struggled to breathe between strokes.

To his surprise, his wolf was quietly humming with the pleasure she was giving him, but staying buried. After a long delicious minute of this, his sanity returned, and he gently lifted her mouth from where it was greedily devouring him.

"Dammit, woman," he said, breathless. "I told you, I can't do this."

"And I'm going to prove you wrong." She pushed him back on the bed. "Scoot to the head of the bed, soldier."

He grinned, in spite of the fact that she was playing with fire. But his wolf was quiet, at least for the moment.

If it started to claw its way out again, the way it did when Jace had her up against the door, then he would just have to pull away. Sooner, this time.

He edged backward and leaned against the pillows propped at the head of his bed. "What are my orders, Captain?"

She crawled across the bed toward him, her hungry gaze dropping to his cock then springing up to lock him with an intensely sexy look. "Your mission is to see how long you can hold out." When she reached him, she straddled him, poised over his cock, placing it right at her entrance. Her gorgeous breasts were level with his face. She peered down at him with a lascivious smile. "You're also allowed to enjoy the view."

"I'm going to enjoy the hell out of this view." He palmed both of her breasts, bringing one tight nipple to his mouth. Then she quickly sank down on his cock. He groaned, releasing her breast from his mouth and slipping one hand to the small of her back to balance her as she started to ride him. His head tipped back against the headrest for a moment, then he snapped his eyes open again. He wanted to see the pleasure she was taking from him, breasts bouncing before his face, her own head tipped back as her breathing quickened. God, she felt *so* good. He didn't know how far he could take it—his wolf had come out mostly when he was close to his own release—so he needed to get her there *first*. He reluctantly dropped the hold he had on the heavy globe of her breast and slid his hand down to rub her hot little nub.

She gasped when he touched her sex, and he knew that would take her there fast—and him, too. It was so damn sexy, watching his cock disappear into her. He would never be able to claim her, he never be able to sink his fangs into her and make her his mate, but if he could keep his wolf under control, maybe he could keep her with enough of *this*—his love, his protection, and all the hot orgasms she could stand.

"Oh, God, Jace!" she cried out, and he could feel her tightening around him. He breathed through his teeth, trying to forestall his own release, all while flicking his thumb across her nub with one hand and grabbing her breast with the other. He twisted her nipple to give her that small touch of pain to tip her over the edge. She screamed his name and came undone around him, convulsing around his cock, and suddenly, his own climax rushed at him.

*No, no, no...* but it was there, coursing white-hot pleasure through him, more intense than anything he'd felt before. Through the blinding haze of release, he could tell—*he was still human*. He groaned with relief and pleasure as she rode the last waves and then collapsed on him, burying him in the softness of her arms and her breasts in his face, wrapped around him, kissing him.

He rolled to the side with her, both of them collapsing with their pleasure spent. She cuddled into him— complete trust, complete openness, every small part of her spread wide to him. It was the most sublime feeling he'd ever known, and he couldn't stop touching her, all over, just skimming his hands and reveling in her nearness. Her soft kisses were slowing, and a drowsy haze was calming his motions, too. They remained locked together, tangled but utterly comfortable in each other's arms.

She nibbled up his neck to his ear and whispered, "I told you so."

He huffed a small laugh. She was right—he'd kept his wolf contained—but he had no idea if it would happen the next time. Or the next. He couldn't be sure of any of it. But at the moment, all he cared about was the soft whisper of her skin against his.

He held tight onto the warmth of her against him, and before he knew it, he was swiftly tumbling into sleep.

# CHAPTER 12

Piper's eyes were still closed when the sun moved onto her face. She squinted her eyes open and peered at the window—the sun's early morning glory was blazing through. Jace's arms were wrapped around her, still spooning her from behind and draping his arm and leg across her body in the most delicious blanket she would ever have.

She was *so* in love with this man. Last night had been amazing—hot sex, revealed secrets, and the thrill of making him come without unleashing that wildness he didn't think he could control.

He was so wrong about there being an evil part of him, something that killed people. She knew with absolute certainty, deep in her being, that Jace River was nothing but good, through and through. There is no way his beast had done anything like what he believed. She had no idea what the real story was behind his time in Afghanistan, but she knew the fog of war clouded the sharpest minds. *Something* had happened to him over there, and once she found Noah and the other shifters, she would get to the bottom of it.

She had never wanted a mate—the very idea still curled knots of tension inside her stomach—but when she looked at this beautiful man lying next to her, sleeping soundly on his bed, she saw possibilities that had never been open to her before. She'd never wanted anyone the way she wanted him. The idea of submitting still ran shudders through her mind and her body—it was a complete domination, as far she could tell. Her father, the Colonel, certainly had used every ounce of magic to dominate her mother and turn her into an empty shell of a woman. But Piper couldn't imagine Jace ever doing anything like that, especially to a woman he cared for and loved.

*He said he wanted to love her.* She could tell by the look in his eyes when he said it that he didn't mean the hot sex, the driving of his cock into her body which he held out as a reward for her staying in his arms. He meant he wanted to give her his *heart*—something she still could hardly believe. It was like a fantasy come to life.

Jace made a soft breathy sound, like he was rising up from the depths of his sleep. It killed her that he refused to take a mate. Not that it should be *her*—the idea still ran shivers through her—but he deserved everything that was good in this world, and for Jace River, having a mate was one of those things. In the end, if she could cure him of this belief that his wolf was dangerously wild, and she was still too afraid to submit to him herself, then she would have to let him go. Make sure he was free to claim a mate who deserved everything that he was.

Jace stirred, his hands sweeping across her body and sending an echo of the delicious pleasure he'd given her multiple times. He yawned and slowly opened his eyes. He blinked at her, then suddenly jerked out of bed, scrambling away from her. His chest rose and fell rapidly, and he stared at her with wild eyes.

"We fell asleep!" he panted.

"Well, you did wear me out, soldier." She gave him a

sexy grin that she hoped would be an invitation for him to come back to bed and give her more reasons to be tired.

But he just shook his head and ran his hand through his hair. "I told you… I have nightmares." His hand stilled, his face paled. He scanned her naked body with a critical, unpassionate eye, as if looking for injuries. "My wolf comes out at night."

"I told you—you would never hurt me."

He rubbed both of his hands over his face and took a deep breath. Then he shook his head and slowly climbed back into bed with her. "We have to be more careful than that. I *really* can't control it at all when I'm sleeping." He gestured to the door. "I don't have a lock on there for nothing."

She touched her fingertips to his face and gazed into his eyes. Her touch seemed to calm him. Her wolf was practically purring inside her with just that small connection.

"I know you don't believe it," she said. "But I know your wolf would never hurt me. Someday, I'm going to prove it to you."

He leaned in to kiss her, softly and gently, then pulled back. "I'm broken, Piper. If you'll have me, at least for now, I'll take whatever you'll give." He kissed her again, snuggling in closer, pressing their naked bodies to one another. His morning erection was calling to her hand, so she reached down to stroke it. He pulled her hand away.

"Maybe later," he said. "We have to get up sometime."

She pouted, and it wasn't much of an exaggeration. Her body couldn't get enough of his.

He gave her a bashful look, dipping his chin and looking up at her through his lashes. "I meant everything I said last night… but I didn't know you didn't want a mate. Or maybe that you think you shouldn't because of what happened to your mother. But I want you to know that you *should,* someday. If you find someone you want. You shouldn't deny yourself that. I'll always protect you, no matter what. Everyone should have someone in their corner, and I'm that for you. Forever. Whether I can have you in my bed, or not, is just an extremely awesome potential bonus." He gave her a small smile. "But I will admit that the idea of another man's hands on you at the moment could actually turn me into a homicidal maniac. In human form."

She grinned. Jace had already ruined her for all other men, and he didn't even know it. She looped her leg over his hip, bringing her still-damp core closer to his still-hard erection. "There is only one man's hands I want on me right now, only I can't seem to get him to put them in the proper place." All this talk of mates they couldn't have just made her more determined to prove to him that his wolf was good.

He groaned, a sexy frustrated sound, and slid his hand between her legs, making her gasp.

"I'd like nothing more than to play with your body all day," he whispered against her skin between rapidly speeding up breaths. "But we really do need to get downstairs and be ready to move, in case the coven comes through for us."

Piper pulled in a deep breath, kissed him hard, and then wrenched her body away from his. Her wolf growled her disapproval. "You really are no fun at all, Jace River." But she was joking, because he was absolutely right—finding Noah took precedence over everything else. And she loved that he was staying on target with that.

They quickly dressed, but she had to fight a massive surge of lust again when Jace insisted that they shower together for "maximum efficiency." It *did* get them downstairs sooner, if a lot less satisfied.

Jared was already in the kitchen, scarfing down eggs and bacon and toast. He looked utterly unsurprised to see them stumbling in together, hand-in-hand, hair still wet from the shower. He grunted a kind of "good morning" acknowledgment and finished off his plate. While he rose up to clean his plate, Jace dug out some eggs and cheese from the refrigerator and proceeded to cook in front of her eyes.

"Are you kidding me?" she asked, eyes wide. "You're saying that you cook *as well?*" She meant *in addition to* being extremely hot in bed—and every other fine feature the man had—but she wasn't going to say all that in front of Jared.

Jace just grinned, not breaking stride as he cracked the eggs and sent sizzling sounds and smells of deliciousness throughout the kitchen.

Piper tap Jared on the elbow, catching him before he left the kitchen—he jerked back in surprise at the touch. She frowned and wondered if Jace was the only River brother with some kind of dark secret. Jared had the look of a haunted man, and it didn't seem to be just his personality, like some people were. Piper had learned to judge people quickly in the field, sizing them up by their facial tics and their verbal and nonverbal responses, even in the most innocuous of situations. Jared was a man who was carrying something deep inside him, a burden he didn't think he could ever put down, so he took it with him everywhere.

"I was just wondering," she said, with a forced lightness, "if you'd had any more luck in finding Agent Smith?"

He shook his head, frowning. "No, but I've been thinking about what you said last night, about the Senator and his plans to register shifters. That's something that can't happen."

"It absolutely can happen," Jace said from the stovetop, where he was almost finished with the eggs. "Politicians are sick bunch—they will happily put people at risk, destroy lives, and ruin businesses, all for a few more votes. And to hold onto their power."

Piper just stared at Jared because even though Jace misunderstood, she knew exactly what Jared was saying. That it *couldn't happen*—meaning that Jared wouldn't let it happen. She didn't know what that meant to him, but she could see the cold determination in his eyes.

"Maybe," she said, carefully, "if we can find the missing shifters, and my brother, Noah, we'll find something on the Senator as well. Something that will shut him down."

Jared nodded, still holding her in an intense gaze. "That's our top priority. Rescuing your brother and the others. We'll do that first." Then he turned and strode from the room.

Piper shivered a little in the cold wake he left behind.

Jace didn't seem to notice, just plated up their eggs and grabbed some juice from the refrigerator. They sat down to eat, and silence fell over them as they scarfed down the food. She was *ravenous*—strong night of sex tend to do that to her, and doubly so with the emotional tornado she had spun through.

Just as they were finishing up, Jaxson and Olivia flew through the front door, their shoes pounding on the polished wooden floor on their way to the kitchen.

"Oh good, you're up!" Jaxson gushed. "We've got a line on your brother, Piper."

She jerked up from the table. "You do?"

"My aunt Gwen is *so* much a better witch than I am," Olivia said with a grimace. "It's kind of ridiculous that I even *think* I can do magic compared to what she does."

Piper didn't care about any of that. "Where is he?"

"There's an abandoned airfield on the outskirts of Seattle." Jaxson turned to Jace. "Lots of empty hangars.

Sound familiar?"

Jace nodded. "Easy access, in and out. No reason for anyone to stop by. Perfect for conducting experiments that no one will ever see. Sounds like the kind of place Agent Smith would hang out."

"The only problem is the place is *huge.*" Jaxson shook his head. "We know exactly which hangar they're in, assuming the coven's magic is good and has pinpointed the right coordinates, but it's wide open."

Jace grimaced. "If I were Agent Smith, I'd have security all around the perimeter. Lots of warning, so no one can get close. Especially since we've already crashed his party once."

"Exactly." Jaxson hooked a thumb over his shoulder. "I'll go round up some of the pack and get ready to roll. We need to move fast."

Piper agreed emphatically, she didn't understand the source of their urgency. "Why?"

Jaxson frowned. "It already took us an hour to get here from downtown. It'll take at least another hour to reach the airfield. I don't want them slipping away again."

Piper nodded quickly, and Jaxson and Olivia hurried out of the room.

Jace turned to her. "You want to go, don't you?"

Piper snorted. "Besides the fact that you guys could use my tactical knowledge, I'd like to see you try to stop me."

Jace grinned and slid his hands up along her shoulders, to her neck, and all the way up to hold her cheeks with just his fingertips. He kissed her lightly. "You know, you turn me on when you talk like that."

She smirked. "And I wasn't even trying."

He kissed her softly again. "I know. That's the best part." He pulled back, and a frown settled on his face. "But I actually don't like the idea of you coming along. I don't want to see you in any kind of danger. Ever."

"You're not going all *overprotective alpha* on me, are you?" She looked up into his eyes with a saucy stare that dared him to even think about trying to use an alpha command on her.

"Yeah," he said, softly. "I think maybe I am."

The look he was giving her was the kind that reached inside her—past all the walls she had carefully built over her entire life to keep everyone out—and stirred the deepest parts of her. She dropped her voice, and said softly in return, "I'll be careful. I always am."

He kissed her gently on the forehead, and it almost brought tears to her eyes. "Make sure that you do."

And without him saying it in so many words, she got the message loud and clear—if something happened to her, Jace would feel responsible, just like he felt responsible for those people in the village, whether that was really his fault or not. It made her even more determined to uncover the truth about that, but she also realized that she held another sacred duty in her hands—she needed to not only find her brother, she needed to survive as well.

Because she was not going to be the person who broke Jace River's heart.

# CHAPTER 13

Jace was riding shotgun while Piper drove the black sedan that belonged to his pack.

They were riding across the broken asphalt road at the perimeter of the abandoned airfield where her brother, Noah, and the other shifters were being held. At least, that was what the witches claimed, although he was inclined to believe them. The pack had hastily pulled together a plan that was fraught with risk, undermanned, and really just a bad idea. But they didn't have a lot of options at this point. They could wait and try at a later time, after gathering more intel, but that would just give Agent Smith another chance to slip away. Especially now that the Colonel knew Piper was on to him, and they were about to test just how involved he was in this whole scheme. Jace wouldn't put anything past the man— anyone who abused his family would do anything he could get away with, if it served his purposes.

Jace was still riding high on the fact that Piper wasn't letting the Colonel jerk her around and intimidate her anymore—and that she had opened up to him. The night they spent together, even if that was all there ever was to it, was worth all the risk. He *didn't* like the fact that the two of them were about to volunteer themselves for capture.

"There's the shack." Jace used his miniature scope to check it out, even though they were still a half-mile way. "Looks like just a single guard."

Piper nodded and swung the car onto the long drive that would lead up to the shack. She adjusted her collar where the hidden microphone was sewn into the fabric. "Testing, testing. Can you still hear me, Jaxson?"

His brother was waiting with the rest of the pack farther out along the perimeter, at the opposite side of the airfield. Jace and Piper were supposed to gather intel on security without raising alarms. Well, without raising whatever alarms would happen when they showed up—which would be pretty much all of them. They hoped. That was part of the point. Flush them out, see what they had, then come in for the assault from a different angle, that hopefully, they wouldn't be expecting.

If the witches' magical GPS was correct, the objective was a large hangar in the middle of the airfield. There were several smaller hangars strung out along the length of the single lane airstrip that was crumbling and weed-filled from years of disuse. There were no visible planes in the area, but that probably just meant they were stashed in one of the smaller hangars.

"I hear you loud and clear, Piper," Jaxson's voice came over the stereo speakers in their car. They had it tuned to a far-band frequency that was unlikely to be used by Agent Smith's forces on the airstrip. The communication would be one-way once they left the car, but they were at the maximum distance from the pack right now—if Jaxson could hear them at this point, he should be still receiving once they were inside.

"Do you have a visual on us?" Jace asked his own hidden microphone embedded in his shirt. The car was tricked out with a couple cameras, and he and Piper also carried button ones as well. But the best intel would be whatever movement happened on the airfield once they made their presence known.

"Affirmative. I have a clean line of sight all the way to the hangar." Jaxson's voice was calm. He was the lookout, while the rest of the pack were strategically placed in three different camps around the perimeter, fully armed, and waiting for the signal for the assault. Jaxson would coordinate and lead the assault, but it was up to Jace and Piper to get him the intel he needed for it to be successful.

"All right," Jace said. "I'm going radio silent with the car stereo. Repeat, we will not be able to hear you from here on out. Please don't forget to come get us."

"Well, don't be all day about it," Jaxson said. "I've got a lunch date with Olivia."

Piper smirked and smacked the off button on the radio. "How long have they been together?"

"About six minutes." Jace returned her smile and thought about how fast Piper had whirled into his life as well. "But so far they seem fabulously happy." Jaxson could still hear them, but Jace wasn't saying anything his brother didn't already know. Besides, there wasn't much

Jace would keep from him.

They were coming up on the guard shack. Just a hundred more feet.

"Are they mated?" Piper gave him a sideways look, then kept her eyes on the road.

"Yeah." Jace grimaced. "I didn't know Jaxson couldn't have a mate until after it was all over. He kept it secret for a long time." He watched her carefully to see if she would probe for more.

"Am I the only one who knows *your* secret?" She was sneaking looks at him again, not watching the road. They were almost there.

"Just you, me, my brothers, and the entire United States government—or at least the ones involved in the tribunal in Afghanistan."

She just nodded, and there was no more talking possible, due to the fact that they'd arrived at the shack stationed next to the chain-metal gate that surrounded the airfield. It wasn't the kind that would keep out any serious attempt at infiltration, more a demarcation with an "Off Limits, Private Property" warning hung on it to keep out the curious and the idle.

The guard was dressed in desert camouflage, with an M-16 looped around his shoulder. He was either military or ex-military, but either way, he meant business. And he wasn't pleased to see them arrive, according to his stiff gait as he approached.

Piper threw him a sexy grin, and even though Jace knew it was all for show, he couldn't help having a twinge of jealousy. She had to deploy all her assets on the job, and he was getting a chance to watch her in action, but he wasn't sure how he felt about that. In general? Very hot. Specifically, today? He didn't like it at all.

"This airfield is closed, ma'am." The guard's voice was gruff, as if that might dissuade them more than the gun. Or perhaps convince them he would use it.

"Well, I'd imagine so," Piper said with a smirk. "But we're here to see the secret hangar where you're hiding the shifters. Colonel Wilding sent us." She beamed a faux-innocent smile at him.

The guards face opened in surprise, but it didn't take more than two-tenths of a second for his rifle to come up and point at her head. "Step away from the car!" His boots scuffed the ground as he stumbled back.

Jace held in his growl. He had to play this cool, or it wasn't going to work, but he didn't like a gun pointed at her, no matter what. Piper already had her hands up, but she had to reach down to open the car door.

"Hey, hands in the air!" the guard shouted.

"Well, *Hot Stuff with a Rifle*, I can't really do both, now can I?" Her voice was dead-on sexy and teasing, and Jace couldn't hold back his smirk.

On second thought, he kind of liked watching her work.

Jace's hands were already in the air as well. "Can I stay in the car, too?" he shouted, just to prod the startled guard a little more.

The man's snarl was clear even from ten feet away. His rifle point wavered uncertainly between Piper and Jace.

"Stay right where you are!" The guard stumbled backward toward the shack, obviously changing his mind about the protocol.

Jace and Piper kept their smiles and their hands in the air and waited.

"Do you think this idiot can actually get us inside the airfield?" Piper asked out of the side of her mouth.

"Well, not if you flummox him anymore. Take it easy on the guy, Piper. He's probably only human."

She bit her lip in a way that made him want to bite it himself.

"Hey, knock it off," he said. "I don't want to be

sporting wood when they come to take me away in handcuffs. Could be embarrassing."

She tried to keep in her laugh, but her shoulders were shaking. The guard was on his short-wave radio, gesturing furiously at the car with his gun. It took a few minutes, but eventually a Jeep pulled out of a distant hangar and rumbled down the cracked concrete toward them.

"I hope you're seeing this, Jaxson," Jace said quietly. "Jeep at twelve o'clock, sourced from the small hangar next to the target." He had stowed his binoculars already, but by squinting through the afternoon sun, he could see at least four figures in the military-camouflaged vehicle. "I see two thugs and two suits." He flicked a glance at Piper.

She was keeping her eyes on the nervous guard. "Copy that."

The chain-metal gate rumbled on some mechanical servo that pulled it aside as the Jeep approached. The vehicle stopped on the far side of the gate, even though it was open. Two men in desert camouflage spilled out, followed by two men in dark suits. The paramilitary guys hustled toward them.

"I've got eyes on Agent Smith," Jace whispered,

mostly for Piper's knowledge, but also in case the cameras and Jaxson's scope missed it. "He's the tall one. Unknown suit accompanying him."

The thugs reached their car, and with a flurry of shouts and commands, they ordered Piper and Jace face down onto the dirt-packed road. Jace couldn't see Piper any longer, given she had to exit on the opposite side, which coiled up tension in the pit of his stomach. While the thug shoved a boot in the middle of his back, holding him down, a prick of pain in his shoulder sparked alarm through him. He twisted around to see the thug pocketing a syringe—whatever he injected into Jace didn't take effect right away, but immediate drugging wasn't one of the contingencies they'd planned for.

Jace strained to see where the suits were going. Agent Smith was saying something to Piper, but Jace couldn't make out the words. Just as the thug none-too-gently hauled him to his feet, Agent Smith strolled around the car. His face was full of red fury, no doubt from whatever line Piper had fed him.

"What are you up to, Mr. River?"

"About six-foot-two. Yourself?"

"Whatever game you're playing here, I want you to understand: I'm going to win it." He narrowed his eyes at

Jace. "And my multimillion dollar research project could use another guinea pig. Nice of you to volunteer."

"I just can't get enough of your charm, Agent Smith."

Agent Smith looked seriously unimpressed. He lifted his chin to the thug standing closest Jace, who then sideswiped the butt of his gun across Jace's face. Pain exploded across his cheek, and his head whipped to the side so hard, it spun him to the ground. He tasted blood, but he was sure Agent Smith was just warming up. Shifters healed fast, which meant they could take quite a beating… and Jace already knew Agent Smith liked to mete those out from when he got his jollies with Jaxson strapped to a chair. Watching that go down had been painful, but Jace would happily take whatever Agent Smith had to dish out as long as he didn't start in on Piper. If he did, there was going to be a problem. Namely that Jace wasn't sure he could keep himself under control.

At least the two of them were still conscious— whatever the thugs had injected into them wasn't knocking them out. Which meant it was probably more of the drug Agent Smith had used before to keep them from shifting.

"Bring them," Agent Smith barked. The scuff of his hard-soled shoes meant he was done with Jace for the moment. One of the thugs cuffed his hands behind his back and hauled him up from the ground. He shoved Jace toward the back of his own car, which had been commandeered by the second thug. Agent Smith was returning to the Jeep, while the other suit had Piper by the arm, climbing into the back seat. He pulled Piper into his lap, holding a gun conspicuously pressed against her side. Her hands were cuffed behind her, forcing them into the suit's lap… which Jace was sure the suit was getting off on. The thug guarding Jace shoved him in next to them in the back while he took a seat up front. He kept his pistol trained on Jace's head.

Piper squirmed a little in the suit's lap. "It's getting a little *stiff* in here. Do you like what you're feeling, G-man?" Piper's sultry tone just reddened the suit's face, which would have made Jace laugh… except then the man gave her a vicious leer behind her back and moved his gun to obviously caress Piper's breast.

"I'm kind of hoping you'll misbehave, Ms. Wilding."

Piper huffed with disdain. "Don't get your hopes up, shorty. I don't misbehave for men in cheap suits."

The unnamed agent growled and jabbed his gun deeper into Piper's chest. "Keep talking and we'll see."

Jace's wolf was clawing to come out, and they hadn't

even gotten within a mile of how bad this could go.

"Tell me again why I agreed to this?" he asked Piper, not exactly blowing their cover, but he couldn't help letting her know he was seething with *dislike* about this whole thing.

"Because Daddy ratted these guys out, remember, pumpkin?" Her strained smile had a definite *what the fuck are you doing?* look to it. But Jace didn't think it mattered—they were rambling toward the hangar, regardless. Nothing they said at this point would matter.

"I know, but he didn't mention anything about handcuffs," Jace said, straining to keep his voice light. "Is it too late to mention I'm not into the kinky stuff?"

"Shut up." The front-seat thug nudged Jace's head back with the barrel tip of his gun.

Jace glared at him, but followed Piper's lead and kept quiet for the rest of the ride in. As they were hustled into the main hangar, Jace hoped Jaxson was still getting a good feed on the audio, as well as the button cameras— and that he'd get his ass in here if things went badly for Piper.

Jace tried to twist around, giving his brother a solid look at the inside of the hangar, but it wasn't anything good—dozens of paramilitary types, even more staff in medical scrubs, and at least fifty shifters in cages and strapped to gurneys in miniature medical suites. Where had they all come from? There couldn't be this many that had gone missing from Seattle. Were they bringing in others from around the country?

Suddenly, Piper broke free of the suit holding her and rushed forward—what the hell? Jace's guard whipped his weapon to point straight between Jace's eyes.

"Not a muscle," the man said coolly.

Jace was stuck watching as the suit scrambled after Piper... but she stopped suddenly in front of one of the cages.

"Noah!" she said, then reared back to kick the cage door. "Noah, wake up!" She slammed her shoulder against the metal bars, rattling the entire thing, then the suit reached her and pulled her back.

Jace wanted to go to her, calm her down, but the beefy man guarding him looked like he was waiting for any excuse to put a bullet in Jace's brain.

"No!" That was Piper again. She was on the ground.

"Piper!" Noah, her brother, staggered to the gate of his cell and banged it. "Get the fuck off my sister!"

Piper struggled against the suit's hold, but three guards descended on Piper and pinned her. They hauled her up and held her off the ground, kicking and screaming, and carried her toward one of the medical suites. Agent Smith stood there, a grin slowly spreading across his face.

*No, no, no!*

Jace looked straight in the face of the man holding a gun to his head. "This is not exactly going to plan," he said to him... but he was really speaking to Jaxson.

The guard smirked. "You'll get your turn, shifter." He stepped to the side but didn't lower the weapon. "Come on."

He ushered Jace toward the med suite where Piper was being strapped to a gurney.

*Come on, Jaxson.* Jace didn't know if his brother could get here before they started doing things to Piper that Jace would never forgive himself for. She was putting up a hell of a fight, but they were quickly getting her strapped in. Jace was ticking through the options—head-butt the guard, take his gun, chop him to the neck, somehow call attention to himself, *anything*—but they all had nearly zero chance of success. Just as he was getting ready to do something foolish and very unlikely to work, a smattering of gunfire froze everyone in the hangar.

Then all hell broke loose.

Five different doors around the edges of the hangar

banged open and members of his pack flowed in like black-armor-clad demons. Gunfire erupted everywhere. Jace took that moment of chaos to head-butt his guard then swipe his feet out from under him. He hit the ground hard, but Jace was already gone, turning toward the medical suite where Piper was being held. The melee going on around him gave him cover, but just as he reached her and plowed into one of the guards standing near her, a series of small explosions made him involuntarily duck. A quick glance around showed Jaxson and his pack doing the same while everyone else— guards, medical staff, even Agent Smith, hitting the deck and scrambling for something, like they'd lost some treasure hidden among the crates of supplies.

Then something drifting down caught Jace's gaze—a pinkish cloud was falling on them. He sucked in a breath and worked desperately at getting Piper's restraints off with his hands cuffed behind his back. Her eyes were wide, watching the pink mist fall down around them. She held her breath, too, but Jace wasn't fast enough. And the guard he had just sent the floor with his blow was back up… now with a gas mask on.

He pointed a gun at Jace's head.

Jace stopped his frantic attempt to free Piper. But he

was running out of air... and the pinkish mist was seeping into every pore of his body, tugging on his eyelids, and sending him crashing down into oblivion.

# CHAPTER 14

Piper slowly awoke to the sound of someone being hit. She supposed she should be glad it wasn't *her*—but when she creaked her eyes open and peered through the steel bars of her cage, she almost wished she was the one taking the blows. Jace was tied to a chair, with his hands bound by zip ties around the back, and he was being pummeled by the man he had called Agent Smith. There was no question that Smith was some kind of government operative, judging by the cheap suit and the overabundance of swagger, not to mention the smirk, as he pounded his fist into Jace's face again. Piper had no idea how long this been going on, but Jace was keeping quiet during Agent Smith's barrage of fists and questions. Which meant he was getting worn down.

"I could do this all day," Agent Smith sneered. "Or you could just tell me how many of your pack are still roaming around free. And the location of your safehouse. We can always use a few more volunteers."

"How many volunteers do you need?" Jace asked, but his voice was weary. "You must really suck at science. Otherwise, you wouldn't need so many test subjects, would you?"

Agent Smith plowed his fist into Jace's stomach, and Jace huffed over with the impact. The blow screeched the chair across the floor a few inches, and Jace's hands sprouted claws briefly, then they retracted.

Piper lurched up from the cold concrete floor where she had been lying and grasped hold of the steel bars of the door of her cage. Her stomach was a writhing pit of snakes. She tried to summon her wolf, but the beast was nowhere to be found, somehow hidden in the depths of her mind. Either Agent Smith had injected them with some kind of suppression drug earlier, or the pink mist that had knocked them all out had some kind of anti-shifter medication. Either way, her wolf was silent inside her—which was just wrong. Unnatural feeling. It gave Piper a shudder that ran from the tips of her toes up to lift the hairs on the back of her neck.

Jace must not have gotten the same shot… or maybe his wolf was so powerful, it could resist whatever drug or genetic technology Agent Smith had cooked up.

Piper quickly cased the situation around her. She was locked in a cage by herself, but dozens of cages were stacked around the enormous hangar. She strained to look for Noah, but she couldn't find him. On her left was an empty cage and on the right was a cage holding a man she didn't know. He seemed about the same age as Jace, a few years older than her, and he was standing tensely at the door of his cage, gripping the bars and watching Jace get pummeled.

Jaxson and Jared and the rest of Jace's pack had to be here somewhere, but the alignment of the cages made it difficult to see more than a few cages down the row. The man next to her glanced at her, but only briefly—he was drawn back by another smack to Jace's face, this one whipping his head to the side so hard, Piper could hear bones crack. She gasped and almost cried out—but she knew that would do no good. It might even bring more harm to Jace. She knew shifters were tough, but they weren't impossible to kill. And Agent Smith looked like a man who didn't really care if Jace lived or died, experiments or no.

On the opposite side of the hangar, far enough away that she couldn't see it clearly, were several medical suites. Each bed was filled with a shifter strapped to a gurney—some were writhing around, others were lying still. Piper couldn't tell if they were conscious or not. But then her attention snapped to a tall, powerful figure strolling across the open center of the hangar.

*Her father.*

She knew he had to be involved somehow, but the shock of seeing him *here* still felt like ice running through her veins. Noah was in one of these cages, and now so was she. How could the man even begin to justify that to himself? Maybe he didn't give a fuck about her, but Noah was his own flesh and blood.

The Colonel strolled up to Agent Smith and waved him off from delivering another pounding to Jace's face.

The pause in the beating made Jace looked up. "It's like an asshole parade around here."

The lift in Jace's voice made Piper's heart soar. He

must not be too badly injured if he was giving shit to the Colonel. Agent Smith put his hand on his holstered pistol like he wanted to pull his weapon and kill Jace and have it done with.

Piper gripped the bars of her cage so hard, her skin squeaked against the metal.

"Don't do anything stupid," the Colonel said to Agent Smith, who just growled in response and kept his hand on his weapon. "You're not going to get any more information out of Mr. River, and I'd like to see how he performs under the drug trial. He's a very interesting case."

Agent Smith snarled again, but he pulled a knife from the back of his desert fatigues and advanced towards Jace. Piper was afraid he might just slit Jace's throat, but Smith only cut the zip ties holding Jace's feet to the chair legs, freeing him to stand. Two guards grabbed hold of Jace's arms, one on either side, while Smith cut the ties at his wrists. Then the guards hauled Jace toward the cage next to Piper. Agent Smith turned on his heel, snorting in disgust, and strode toward the medical suites.

The Colonel followed the guards and Jace, watching him struggle to keep his legs underneath him while the paramilitary thugs tossed him in his cell. Piper vaguely noticed the man in the cell next to her—he shuffled away to the far edge, no doubt wanting to keep his distance from this freak show. Once Jace's cell door was locked, the Colonel turned to face her.

"I tried to warn you, Piper, but you never did listen to me. You always had to find the deepest trouble you could get into, didn't you?" His dark eyes stared hard at her.

She returned his glare. "I knew you were a monster, but even I didn't think you were capable of this. How can you not care about your own son?"

"Noah is serving his country now in a way that only a shifter could. If I could've found a way to get *you* into the program sooner, I would have, but you insisted on being out of the country in obscure locations most of the time."

"Sorry to inconvenience you." But she still didn't understand what he meant, and why he'd be willing to sacrifice Noah to his ambitions in such a glaringly obvious way. "What are the Feds doing here? And what are they doing to the shifters?"

"Nothing they didn't volunteer for. Including your brother."

"Somehow, I find that hard to believe."

"It's true. You can ask him yourself." The Colonel had

a twisted kind of pride on his face.

Piper snarled. "He would've told me if he was planning to enter some dark program for shifters in the military. You must've tricked him into it."

"There was a small deception, I will admit. I needed to know if he was even qualified for the program first. I told him it would only be a day or two to travel the center in Afghanistan where we were processing soldiers. But when he tested so well—his blood an ideal match for many of our other test subjects—well…" The Colonel shrugged. "That's when he had an opportunity to serve his country like he never had before."

"You mean that's when it became *involuntary.*" Piper could too easily see Noah not telling her that he was following the Colonel's command for a special assignment. Especially if it was Top Secret. She would disapprove and try to talk him out of it—and probably go straight to the Colonel to complain, getting Noah busted even more. She wished like crazy he had trusted her… and given her a chance to warn him. Noah probably thought he was protecting her. *Damn him.*

"What have you done to all these people?" She gestured at the dozens of cages. "And what the hell makes you think you can get away it?"

"I don't have to *get away with* anything," the Colonel said with a smirk. "This research is fully sanctioned at the highest levels of power." He leaned closer to the bars. "And they're not all shifters, Piper. At least, not yet." He leaned away. "You might be able to help with that, once we have a chance to test your blood to see if you're a good match."

She frowned. "You taking shifter blood and... What? Injecting it into ordinary humans?" *What the hell was her father doing?* Creating new shifters?

"On the modern battlefield, there are no weapons that are off-limits," the Colonel said, puffing out his ridiculously-decorated chest, a full battalion of medals that he kept on display at all times. "Genetic warfare is the latest stealth weapon of choice, and we're not going to win unless we're willing to go as far as the enemy goes. And a little bit further."

"You mean you're willing to do whatever's necessary to rise up in the ranks and earn more chest candy?" All this talk of the battlefield and patriotism was bullshit. She knew her father. This was serving his ambition in some way.

"Disabling enemy shifters is just as important as creating our own shifter fighting force," the Colonel said with a sneer. "And that kind of technology doesn't come without a price."

"One you're happy to have other people pay." Her loathing for him couldn't possibly run any deeper. She was tempted to reach through the bars and scratch his face, but then she remembered she couldn't shift at all.

"Once Senator Krepky has his registration laws in place, it will be even easier to identify possible contributors to the cause." Her father lifted one eyebrow. "Although I suspect, being in the Senator's office frequently, you already knew that was in play. Now that you're here, you'll get to see, up close and personal, how the whole program is going to work. When all's said and done, I'm really quite pleased to see you here, Piper. Maybe I'll finally have some use for you, after all."

She just shook her head—she'd run out of words for the horror that was her own father. "We *will* stop you," she said finally, even if she had no idea how that would happen at the moment.

The Colonel laughed. "Given that you're in a fairly small cage, Piper, you might want to learn how to cooperate for once." Then he turned his back on her and strolled toward the medical suites, probably joining up with his minion Agent Smith for more diabolical planning.

Whatever he intended to use her for, she sure as hell wasn't going to *cooperate*.

The sound of Jace's feet dragging across the floor of his cell drew her attention. "I would have helped you out with telling him off," he said with a small smile, "but you were doing such a magnificent job all on your own."

She hurried to him and reached through the bars to touch his face. He was bruised and cut and battered, but she could already see it starting to heal. "You were doing a pretty fine job yourself with Agent Smith." She dropped her gaze to his hands as they reached through the bars to hold her waist and pull her closer. She pressed her face between the bars and lightly kissed him. Then she whispered, "I saw what you did out there. *Your claws came out.*"

He pulled back, releasing her. "I could barely keep my wolf contained."

Her eyes went wide. "Why did you even try? I wanted to give them both a slash to the face."

He frowned. "One raging wolf isn't going to get us free. Especially one I can't control. We need a real plan to have any hope of escape, much less managing to get everyone out. A lot of these wolves are sick."

A voice spoke from behind her. "A lot of them are dying."

Piper turned to look—it was the man in the cage next to hers.

Jace peered around her. *"Owen?"* His voice had hiked up, astonished. "What… how… holy shit, man, *you're alive!"*

His shock made Piper examine the man—Owen—more closely. He was definitely around Jace's age, late twenties, but his cheeks were hollowed out and dark circles haunted his eyes.

"Who *are* you?" she asked.

"Owen Harding, Private First Class," he said wearily, leaning against the bars. "Last seen serving with Army Specialist Jace River in Afghanistan before our Jeep blew up and the world went to hell."

Piper's mouth dropped open.

# CHAPTER 15

"How is this even possible?" Jace's mind was a whirlwind of confusion. His fellow grunt, Owen, was standing in the cage across from Piper's when he was supposed to be dead.

Although he did *look* halfway to the grave. "The last thing I ever wanted was to see *you* show up here, Jace," Owen said with a tight expression. "They told us you were dead, but I'd always hoped you'd made it out somehow. Only I sure wouldn't wish this place on anyone." His Texas drawl was there, just like it had been in Afghanistan when they served together.

"Have you been here all this time?" Jace asked, horrified. "It's been, what, over a year?" He wracked his brain, trying to figure out how this had happened. Owen was supposed to have been blown up by the same IED that threw Jace out of their patrol Jeep—the singular event that hurtled him down this dark path where he couldn't control his wolf and destroyed a village of innocent people.

Owen gripped the steel bars of his cage. "Yeah, I've been in the program for over a year. There aren't many who've been here longer—at least, not many who are still alive."

Jace leaned his head against the bars of his own cage, wishing he could bridge the gap and grip Owen in a manly hug—the members of his patrol were like brothers to him. Owen had been suffering all this time, and Jace had no idea. It reminded him far too much of Jaxson's dark, closely-held secret, and Jace's failure to even know about it, much less help him.

"What have they been doing to you?" Jace asked with a grimace.

Piper stood by, silent, watching them both with wide eyes.

"It's one experiment after another." Owen sighed. "They take my blood and do something to it—I've heard the staff talk about genetic stuff. Then they inject their serums into some hapless civilian. Sometimes it takes, and they turn into... well... some kind of creature. Nothing I'd call a wolf. Sometimes the injection kills them outright. Some of them probably wished they'd died. They get their wish soon enough. It's like the fucking island of Doctor Moreau in here."

Piper had her hand over her mouth, hiding the horror that Jace felt rippling through his entire body.

"What are they after?" Jace asked. "Why don't they just recruit shifters into the Army? It's not like there aren't a bunch of us already willing to serve our country."

"It's much bigger than that," Owen said, a grim look drawing down his already deathly pale face. "This isn't just about the Army, although they definitely want to create some kind of super soldier. They're working on a universal serum, I think—something that can take all the shifter abilities and amp them up, like dialing it up to eleven or some damn thing. I don't really know. All I know is that I've been trapped here for over a year, praying to God that I die before I inadvertently give them whatever it is they want."

Jace's stomach was doing flips—not only because they needed to get out of here, and *fast,* but because no matter what he did, his friend had already suffered more than anyone should. "Owen, man, if I had any idea… I would've come for you sooner. They told me you were all dead."

He nodded, but it was weak, almost a dazed motion. "I figured. At first, I thought for sure someone would come for us. But then time dragged on, and I knew… we were dead, as far as the world was concerned. And would be dead for real soon."

*"Jesus Christ,"* Jace whispered, running his hand through his hair. His chest was tight with the guilt about all of this. "I still don't understand—why did they take you, but not me?"

"It all started with *him."* Owen lifted his chin to point to the medical bay. "Colonel Wilding. He wasn't our CO, but he was behind the whole thing, setting it up. It was a ruse from the start—they wanted an excuse to bring us all into the program. You, me, Wyatt, Anthony—all shifters, all on one patrol. Funny it didn't even occur to us that was strange, huh? The IED was already planted. They sent us to drive over the damn thing, knowing we were shifters, and it probably wouldn't kill us. Colonel

Wilding himself called in the artillery and blew up the village."

*"What?"* Jace gasped. "But they told me… they said that I…" Jace swallowed, just now realizing what Owen was saying—that Jace didn't actually kill all those people in the village. "They told me an animal killed everyone. Said it was the most powerful shifter they'd ever seen… that it was *me*. I didn't remember anything, and I had no reason to think—"

"They lied to you," Owen said. Of course, that was obvious now. "I don't know why they'd make up a story like that, but these guys are covering up all kinds of shit. If I had to guess, Colonel Wilding must've come in for some trouble with targeting that village. Maybe they said it was friendly fire something. I don't know. I've been locked up here ever since. But he's just enough of a bastard to try to pin everything on you, the one shifter he couldn't catch."

"Catch?" Jace asked. "Owen, what happened back there? I really don't remember any of it."

Owen shook his head. "Not much of a surprise your memory's shot, given how much they had to tranq you to even slow you down. When you didn't show up with the rest of us in the program, I thought they just killed you outright. When the IED went off, I was thrown from the Jeep, but you shifted right away, and your wolf went nuts. He took off running toward the village. I chased after, but you were freaking fast, man! By the time I caught up, you were trying to save those villagers. The place had already been bombed, and everything was on fire, a regular inferno. Your wolf dove through those walls of fire, trying to save all those people, like there was nothing to it. Then the troopers swooped in. I thought they were there to help, but then they started shooting at us. I shifted human and tried to explain, but they just took me down with a tranq. Last thing I remember, they were going after you. That crazy wolf of yours just kept trying to save the villagers. If you would've run, I doubt they could've caught you. Wyatt and Anthony didn't see none of it, but I saw you in action. I thought for sure you got away."

Jace glanced at the other cages. "Are they here?"

Owen sighed. "Nope. Dead."

*"Shit."* It was like finding out he had lost them all over again.

"These people are straight-up murderers." Owen's growl finally came out, angry and bitter. "We figured you either escaped or got killed, too. No way had I figured they would just let you go and come back stateside." He shook his head. "But now you're here, just like me, in the end. It's all fucked up, man."

Jace was reeling from the story, but calm was settling deep inside his chest. His wolf was stirring with the memories, and for the first time in a year, that simple fact didn't terrify him.

He glanced at Piper—she had a shine in her eyes that probably reflected the amazement in his.

She gave him a small smile. "You see? You really need to listen to me. I know what I'm talking about." She meant what she said earlier, about him being a good man—words he never would have believed if Owen hadn't seen it all with his own eyes. Jace still had a hard time wrapping his mind around it.

*He didn't kill those people.* It was like a shockwave going through his system, working things loose, reshaping his thoughts, lightening the burden. He had been carrying a rock the size of Mt. Hood, and someone had finally told him he could set it down.

"I don't know what you guys think…" Jace drew in a deep breath and let it out slow. "But I think we should get the fuck out of here. *Now.*"

Piper smiled and reached through the bars to him,

grasping his arm and squeezing. "You can shift. I know you can—I saw you. And we need you, Jace. We need your *wolf.*"

Jace frowned. He had almost shifted in the chair; it was at least possible. He just wasn't sure what would happen after that. He'd blacked out before, in the village, and every time since, whenever he couldn't control himself...

"I don't know if I can control it, Piper," he said quietly. "I've only shifted a few times since Afghanistan. And I never remember it, I just see the damage afterward. Jaxson's had to tranq me a couple times..."

The gleam in her eyes didn't dim. "Things are different now. You know the truth."

Owen had straightened up. "What is she saying? Did they not give you the inhibitor? Holy shit—"

"No, they did," Jace cut him off by holding up a hand. They needed to keep this quiet. "It's just that, for me, I don't think it's enough. I think my wolf might still be able to come out and cause some problems." He grimaced. "I'm just not sure how big of a problem that's going to be. Or if it'll help. We still need a plan."

Piper's smile tempered into a devious look that perked up his wolf, almost like he was drawn to her more dangerous side. The side that probably had experience breaking out of secret prisons. "They use key cards. That's all I need. You shift, get me a card, and keep them occupied with your badass self. I'll do the rest."

He grinned and pulled her close, reaching through the bars to quickly kiss her again. He loved that she believed in him, but the idea of shifting was tying his stomach in knots. "I don't know…"

"Remember how I said you need to listen to me?" she asked, playfully. "Well, you need to listen to me *now*. You can do this. Because even when you were completely out of your mind, you were trying to save people. I told you—you're good to the core, Jace River. You can't help it."

"Heads up," Owen said quietly.

Jace looked up—one of the paramilitary thugs was headed their way, key card in hand.

Piper reached through the bars to kiss him fiercely. "Do it," she whispered.

Jace stepped back from the bars. The guard was coming straight for his cell. Jace closed his eyes briefly— could he really do this? If it all went south, at least Piper was safe in her cage. The others, too. The guards would take him out first—that would be the idea, anyway, as he distracted them—and if he died in a fiery blaze of bullets, at least he would've done all he could. Nothing could make up for leaving Owen in this horror show for a year… except breaking him free. And saving his brothers and Piper and all the others from the same fate.

That was something worth dying for.

Jace opened his eyes just as the guard swiped his key card across the door to his cell.

He glanced at Piper. "Tell my brothers." He wanted them to know the truth about him—she would know what to do.

Then he closed his eyes and summoned his wolf.

# CHAPTER 16

Piper watched as Jace shifted, her mouth dropping open in awe.

It was fast, over in an instant, but in that split second of time, the man she had fallen in love with transformed from a sexy ex-Army Specialist to the most magnificent beast she had ever seen. He was *huge*. Jace had said his wolf was twice the size of a normal one, but that wasn't even close. The wolf stood as tall as the guard who had just swiped open his cage—he could stare the guard in the face, eye to eye. Only the guard's face was slack with shock. Jace's black fur was ragged and bristled out, his fangs bared with drool dripping to the floor in fat drops. A growl started low inside the beast's chest and slowly rumbled up from the depths.

It reached a peak just as the wolf lunged.

The guard was so immobilized by the sight of this enormous creature coming for him that he barely got an arm up to defend himself—and it was the one holding the key card. The wolf clamped his jaws on the guard's arm and shook it. The card went flying, and the man finally screamed as his arm was shredded. The monster wolf barely fit through the narrow door of his cell, and as he surged through, he sent a shudder through the rest of his cage and Piper's as well. He rampaged out into the open space of the hangar between the cells and storage bins, heading straight for the medical suites at the far end. Shouts erupted, and more screams rang out as Jace's wolf disarmed the panic-stricken guards by clamping down on their gun-wielding arms and tossing them like rag dolls against the cages. Piper was momentarily mesmerized by the insane amount of power in Jace's wolf form, the snarling fury of it… but she had a job to do in these precious few seconds he was buying them.

She rushed to the front of her cage and thrust her arm through the bars—the key card was just out of reach! *Dammit.* She yanked off her boot and used that to extend her reach, just barely nabbing the card and sliding it toward her. Jace's wolf had drawn everyone's attention— the few guards who had been loitering near the cages on her side of the hangar had quickly rushed toward the melee of people trying to contain the oversized beast. He was surrounded by a dozen of them now, and several shots rang out across the metal-and-concrete confines of the hangar.

Piper wrenched away from watching him, hurrying to do her part. She quickly swiped open her own door but left it just slightly ajar. Then she rushed to Owen and passed him the card.

"Keep passing it down," she said breathlessly, "and keep it quiet. We need to all spring at once. The last one in the line gives the signal—then we all go. Do it *fast*, Owen." She glanced back at Jace's wolf fighting off attacks from all sides but still moving. "He doesn't have much time."

Owen dashed to unlock his own door and sprinted to the far side of his cell to pass the key card and the message along. There was a long line of cells in Owen's direction. Piper couldn't bridge the gap of Jace's cage next to hers—they would have to liberate those prisoners, as well as the others on the far side of the hangar, separately. But an initial rush of a dozen or so prisoners on the loose should be enough to cause panic… and give them a fighting chance.

If only Jace could hold out that long.

She hurried back to the door of her cell, now slightly ajar, and gripped the bars as she watched Jace's wolf fight for his life—and theirs.

Piper's heart beat loudly in her chest, one steady pound at a time. Jace was getting hit—some of those shots had to find their target—but he was taking them out as well. The guards with guns fared the worst. Their screams as they were slammed against the concrete floor or steel-barred cages echoed throughout the hangar. Several scrambled to get larger rifles. Piper prayed they only held tranq darts… a prayer answered by the whooshing sound they made when they fired. But tranq darts were ineffective against Jace's wolf, just as they had been in Afghanistan… at least so far. The beast charged the men trying to pump more darts into him, scattering them and causing even more panic. He really was a spectacle to behold. She understood why Jace would think such a beast was made for destruction only. But she knew better. Even in this fight, he wasn't killing people— just disabling them, tearing into their arms and knocking them unconscious so they could no longer shoot at him.

Still... shot after shot rang out. A hot tear coursed down Piper's face as she waited, trembling at the door, trapped by this plan of hers to have most of the prisoners free before the guards were aware. She glanced nervously at Owen in the cage next door. He shook his head. *Not yet.* She gripped the bars of the cage harder and gritted her teeth.

She didn't know how much longer she could stand to wait.

If only Jace would just *kill* the men—tear out their throats, so they couldn't keep coming back for more. Pumping more bullets into his body. He was *enormous*— and his hide must be amazingly thick to keep going this long—but he was still taking an enormous beating.

Jace's good nature was going to get him killed.

Her father and Agent Smith cowered in one of the medical suites, hiding behind the gurneys. The shifters who were strapped down were struggling to free themselves.

Jace must've noticed them struggling, too. He lunged

toward the trapped prisoners—or maybe he was going after her father—right when a shout came from the cages. All at once, the doors flung open, and a dozen burly shifter men raced out. Piper burst from her cage as well and sprinted across the open floor as fast as her human legs would carry her. She couldn't shift, just like the other prisoners, but she was heading straight for Jace, determined to get him out of the fight—he'd already taken too many hits. A quick glance behind her showed one of the prisoners staying behind with the key card, rapidly running between the cages and liberating the rest.

The hangar was in complete chaos.

The guards had scattered, no longer focused on containing Jace's wolf, now that the prisoners were roaming free. They were vastly outnumbered, and while most of the prisoners couldn't shift, they made up for it with pent-up rage—a full on melee broke out.

Her father stood, paralyzed with fear, watching as Jace's wolf used his razor-sharp claws to shred the bindings holding the prisoners down. Piper arrived at his side just in time to see her father snap out of his daze and draw his pistol.

Piper shrieked, "Watch out!"

But Jace's wolf was intent on his task and didn't seem

to hear her.

Her father fired, nearly point-blank, and Jace's beast was thrown back by the force of it. He slumped below the gurney, ripping the last shreds of the bindings free. Her father scurried around the metal bed, obviously planning to pump the rest of his bullets into Jace's fallen body, but Piper blocked her father's way. She didn't have claws to rake across his face, but she managed to take him by surprise, scratching at his face with her human hands... and more importantly, she knocked the gun free. It tumbled across the floor. Her father snarled at her and shoved her aside. Then he shifted and lunged at Jace, taking him on, wolf to wolf. Jace was injured—several spots were matted dark with blood on his chest and arms and legs. That was the only reason her father had any chance at all.

But it didn't matter—Jace's wolf howled in rage and rolled her father's wolf form easily. Jace's beast quickly had him pinned, with his massive jaws clamped around her father's throat.

Piper hesitated... her father deserved to die for the things he had done. To her. To Noah. To who knew how many innocent shifters. All because he wanted more power and prestige. He was a terrible, terrible man. But

Jace didn't deserve to be a murderer. She knew how much that would weigh on him, and no matter how much her father deserved it. Piper didn't want Jace to be the one who carried that burden for the rest of his life.

Jace was hesitating, growling and drooling all over her father's neck pinched tight by his fangs. Piper wished she could shift so she could hear his thoughts… but it was obvious he was in turmoil. She slowly approached the giant, snarling beast with her hands up. The chaos around them dimmed. She didn't know where Noah or Owen or either of Jace's brothers were—the entire world telescoped down to just her and Jace and her father's life held in the balance.

Jace's wolf hadn't heard her before—when she warned him—and she wasn't sure if the wolf was in control or Jace was. Or if he would even recognize her words. But she spoke softly as she edged toward him, reaching out a hand. "You don't have to kill him." If he could understand her words, he was probably the only one who could hear her over his own snarls and her father's pathetic whimpering and begging for his life.

Jace's wolf growled at her—not a warning or a threat. Somehow she knew it was a rebuttal—he wanted to end it, right here, right now.

Jaxson appeared out of nowhere with a tranquilizer gun. He pointed it at Jace's neck.

"No!" Piper shouted, turning and holding both hands out to stop him. She moved her body between Jaxson's tranq gun and Jace's wolf. He was already injured, already had who knew how many darts in him. He might not survive another.

"Piper, you don't understand," Jaxson said, but his voice carried heartbreak. "He's not himself. I have to stop him. He would want this."

"He's *not* a wild animal," Piper said, harshly. "He's your brother! And he'll listen to me. I know he will."

Jared appeared at his brother's side, carrying a pistol, but not pointing it at anyone. He quickly scanned the situation. "Let her try, Jaxson. His beast won't harm her."

"You don't know that," Jaxson hissed at his brother. But he hesitated a long moment, then slowly lowered the muzzle of the tranq gun.

Piper turned back to Jace and reached out to the flank of his wolf. "I know you would never hurt me," she whispered to him. His jaws were still tight around her father's neck—his face was turning red. "But you don't have to do this, Jace. The Colonel can never hurt me again. You've stopped him. He's not going to hurt *anyone* again. You don't need to take his life to stop him."

Jace's wolf shook its head, disagreeing with her and digging deeper into her father's throat. The Colonel yelped, an undignified sound, but she ignored it. She worked her fingers into Jace's thick coat, caressing him, petting his wolf, reassuring him with her touch.

He stopped snarling, and a soft whine leaked around his bared fangs.

"It's all right," she said, sliding her hand up to his head and rubbing him behind the ears. His eyes swung to her, large and dark and round—they were so full of soul, it nearly wrenched her heart out of her chest. "I can't have you going to jail, Jace River. I'm staying, and you promised to love me."

Jace's wolf opened his jaws and released her father. In one swift movement, he shifted back to human, and suddenly stood before her, tall and gorgeous and naked, with the most loving look in his human eyes, just like his wolf. She threw herself into his arms. If they weren't still in the middle of *everything,* she would've hauled him off to a dark corner and made furious love to him.

She loved this man so much.

With Jace safely in her arms, Owen appeared out of the crowd and grabbed hold of her father, hoisting him up from the floor and holding a gun to his head. "Make a move, old man, and I'd be happy to put a bullet in you. Consider it payback."

The red drained from her father's face, but Piper couldn't have cared less if he felt threatened. He *should*. Now that the crisis was past, she glanced around the rest of the hangar. The guards were either disabled, lying on the floor clutching their bloody wounds, or also being held at gunpoint by one of the prisoners. Piper scanned the scattered group, looking for Noah. He broke away from menacing a guard and hurried to her side. Jace released her just as her brother arrived, and she hugged him hard.

When she pulled back, she gripped his cheeks in both hands. "Tell me you're okay," she demanded, tears threatening to choke her words.

He gave that silly crooked grin he'd always had. "Now that my big sister is here to rescue me, things are looking up."

Piper shoved him back with both hands. "*You* are such a pain in my ass, little brother!" She had to struggle to chastise him through the tears, shaking a furious finger at him. "Next time you run off to do something stupid, like volunteer for a dark program, let me know first! Do you know how hard it was to track you down?"

Noah shook his head and glanced at Owen holding his father. "I hate it when you're right, Piper. I should've known better."

"Damn straight." She grabbed him and hugged him again.

"But you *do* always bring the party with you, sis." He held her tight, and when she pulled back, he had a smile on his face. He slid a look to Jace. "And your boyfriend is a hell of a fighter." Noah extended his hand, and Jace shook it.

Then Jace paled and braced himself against the gurney, and Piper realized how injured he really was. Blood was weeping from several holes all over his body.

She rushed brace him so he wouldn't fall. "We need a medic!" she yelled out.

"I *am* the medic," he said, weakly. "Just a few holes. Nothing that won't heal up on its own. Probably."

"Probably is *not* good enough." She couldn't tell if he was joking or not, but he looked like he was ready to pass out. Before she could do something about that, a group of four camouflage Jeeps rolled in front of the open hangar door. Piper watched, slack-jawed, as Daniel spilled out of the first Jeep, and a dozen armed Army MPs flowed out of the rest. They hustled into the hangar, weapons at the ready, sweeping the area.

Daniel strode toward her, eyes wide, pistol out, but pointed at the ground. "Piper are you all right—" He cut himself off when he saw Noah standing beside her. *"Noah!"* His voice was disbelieving.

"Hey, bro." Noah threw side look to the Piper, and she shook her head. She wasn't at all sure what Daniel was doing, storming in like this.

Daniel motioned to his MPs, and they took up a perimeter stance around all the prisoners and the downed the guards. Then he stared at the shredded straps of the gurneys, and Jace's blood covered form. "What's going on here?"

That was when he saw their father being held at gunpoint by Owen. Daniel's gun came up and pointed at Owen's head.

"Daniel!" the Colonel exclaimed, holding his throat, which was bloodied from Jace's fangs. The greasiness in her father's voice made Piper wish Owen had decided to shoot him after all. "Thank God, you're here. These criminals had just about beaten us." Behind her father and Owen, two of the other prisoners had Agent Smith on the ground, their boots pressed into his back, holding him still. It was clear the prisoners were in charge—but it was also obvious that they had maimed a lot of people, namely guards, in the process.

Daniel's gun wavered. "Piper, are you responsible for this?"

Piper stood taller. "Yes." And he better not try to undo this escape, or she would find a way to tear out her brother's throat with her own fangs.

Jace reached for her hand. "She's responsible for this, all right. If it weren't for her, there would be a lot more people dead, including your father, who she convinced me not to kill just a minute ago. And probably your brother, Noah, as well, who has been trapped here, tormented by your father and Agent Smith, that asshole on the ground with the boots on his back." Jace pulled in a ragged breath, and Piper's heart clenched—she needed to get a healer for him, *stat*. But they would only be able to do that if Daniel and his MPs were on their side.

"Don't listen to them," the Colonel rasped out, his hand still on his throat, playing up his non-injury. "Daniel, son, you know she's never been anything but trouble. For herself and for everyone else."

Daniel scowled. "Doesn't look that way to me, *Dad*." He turned to Piper. "I went back to the safehouse. This whole thing wasn't sitting right with me. I don't always like the things you do, Piper. I think you're reckless, arrogant, and a danger to others. But…" His gaze flicked to Noah standing next to her. "But the one thing you've always cared about in this world was *him*. When Mrs. River told me you'd found Noah and had convinced the entire pack to go after him… I figured you could probably use a little help."

Piper's shoulders dropped, and she huffed out a sigh of relief. Then a scuffle behind her drew her attention. Her father had quickly disarmed Owen, and now they had reversed positions, with the Colonel holding the gun to Owen's head. In his weakened state, Owen could hardly fight back.

Piper gritted her teeth.

"I'm not going down for this, Daniel," the Colonel growled. Then he raised his voice. "Tell your men to stand down."

Daniel gave him a look of disgust, and he swung his weapon to point at the Colonel's head. "Remember all those times you made me stay on the target range until I finally hit dead-center? Put down the weapon, sir, or you'll find out exactly how good a shot I am."

The Colonel's mouth momentarily fell open, but he

didn't move. "I'm not bluffing, son. And you'll pay for this, once all of this is said and done."

"This is your only warning." Daniel's steely-eyed gaze convinced Piper well enough—he was *actually* going to shoot their father if he didn't stand down.

Piper's eyebrows hiked up, and it seemed like everyone was holding their breath. The Colonel's eyes slowly went wide as he seemed to realize the same thing. He released Owen all of a sudden and threw his hands in the air. Two of Daniel's MPs rushed forward and disarmed her father, shoving him to the ground and cuffing his hands behind his back.

Piper could hardly believe it.

Daniel was putting his own father under arrest.

The prisoners were free.

She'd found Noah.

And even Jace's elusive Agent Smith had been caught.

Then Jace let out a soft groan. His hold on the gurney slackened, and he slumped to the floor, smacking on the concrete.

Piper gasped and dropped down next to him. "We need a healer!" she shouted, tears reaching up to choke her again.

One of the prisoners rushed forward. It was a woman,

and her eyes were sunken and shadowed like Owen's—she must've been imprisoned for a long time.

"Get him up on the gurney," she quickly instructed the others standing around them. A rush of hands gripped Jace's body and heaved him up onto the silver table. Noah and Daniel were among them, along with Jace's brothers, Jaxson and Jared. They stepped back but stayed nearby, watching the woman work. Another prisoner scavenged a needle and thread and medical kit from the nearby cabinets and brought them to her. Jace's eyes were squeezed shut, and his skin was too pale. He looked like he had passed out, but then he moaned when the woman started digging into his wounds.

An arm slipped around Piper, and she realized she was shaking.

She looked up—it was Noah.

"He's strong," her brother said. "And not just his wolf, I have a feeling. I don't know the man at all, but if he's won your heart, he has to be something special."

She was choked up and could hardly force the words out. "He is."

"Then I'm sure he's going to be fine."

Piper prayed her brother was right as she watched the woman pull bullet after bullet from Jace's quivering body and stitch up the battered flesh left behind.

# CHAPTER 17

J ace felt like he'd been attacked by a porcupine with poisoned quills.

At least, that was the vague thought he had as he worked his way up from the depths of sleep. He didn't know who sewed him up, but he wouldn't be alive without them. He'd stayed awake for most of the painful extraction of bullets from his body. He lost count after fourteen, and that didn't even include the darts. Although most of those hadn't made their way into his system. He was convinced the only reason he'd been able to stay conscious as long as he had was that the darts had anesthetized some of the pain—that and massive doses of adrenaline. But the surgery had been too much, and he went down hard, tumbling into a blissful pain-free blackness.

He remembered praying he'd actually wake up again.

Now that he was rousing out of that deep sleep, he realized he must've been transported back to the safehouse. He hadn't opened his eyes yet, but the soft blanket over him, the deep pillow under his head, and the wafting smell of dinner told him he'd made it home alive.

Jace stretched and groaned and finally opened his eyes. The room was very dimly lit by light sneaking under the doorway and through his window. It was nighttime, he was in his bedroom, and the moon glistened everything with a silver sheen. He rolled toward it, letting out a groan because the bullet wounds were still fresh, only to find Piper sitting next to his bed.

A wide grin was plastered on her face.

"Oh, um…" he mumbled. "You're here." Very articulate, Jace. He swallowed and tried to come up with something coherent to say, but his throat was extremely dry.

"Hello, big sexy thing," Piper said with a smirk. She handed him a glass of water that she snatched up from the floor next to his bed. "I'm glad you decided to wake up on my watch. I'd hate for one of your brothers to have the pleasure of that very special greeting."

He propped himself up on his elbow and grimaced through the pain. He took a sip of water before trying to speak again. "Thanks for saving my life." That seemed a little better, and a hell of a lot closer to how he truly felt.

"I'm afraid that honor belongs to that healer girl, Macy." She cocked her head. "I hope that's not a requirement for sticking around."

He smiled. He could hardly believe it—they had found her brother, rescued the others, and he'd lived through the whole thing—best of all, the bad guys had been caught. At least, he hoped so. He had pretty much passed out during the critical part. And his wolf… it still boggled his mind that he'd been wrong all along about that. That Colonel Wilding had let him take the fall for that village. That he wasn't a murderer… and his wolf was something that enjoyed the hell out of Piper scratching him behind the ears. The truly best part was *her,* sitting in a chair at his bedside and looking after him. He didn't know if he could convince her to stay, not really—she had a job that took her all over the world. And she was damn good at it.

But she couldn't have any doubts as to how he felt about her now.

He dipped his head to peer at her. "I've been trying to get you to stick around since you snuck into my house in the middle of the night." He smirked. "In fact, maybe we could go back to the kitchen and start up where we left off."

She gave him a sexy grin and leaned closer. Her simple V-neck was cut low enough to remind him that he hadn't paid anywhere near enough attention to her gorgeous breasts the last time they had made love—which had also been their first time. That was something he planned to remedy one way or the other. *Soon.*

"I don't know, soldier. You sure you're up for those kinds of gymnastics? With the amount of ammo Macy pulled out of your body, you could start your own Army surplus shop."

He handed the glass of water back to her, but as soon as she took it, he snagged her hand and pulled her closer. "How about you come over here, and we find out?"

She set the glass down and crawled into bed with him. His body still ached, but the delicious feel of her sliding into his lap made him forget all about it. Then she kissed him, and his hands got full really fast, holding her back with one to pull her closer and palming her breast with the other.

When she pulled back from the kiss, he said, "Now this is the way to wake up." He kneaded the hot, heavy globe of breast again and went for another kiss, but she stopped him with two fingers to his lips and a serious expression.

He stilled his hands and brought them back to her hips. "What's wrong?"

She shook her head but didn't answer... just looked at his chest, which was apparently left bare after the surgery. It was crisscrossed with fresh scars, shining sliver-pink in the moonlight. She traced one with her fingertip, and all the aches and pains faded in a surge of lust that had his cock rising to the occasion.

But she hadn't answered his question. He gently lifted her hand from his chest, kissed her fingertips one at a time, then curled her hand to rest on him again. "You're not saying what's on your mind, Piper Wilding. And that's just peculiar."

She smiled. "You know me so well, do you? Now that we've been acquainted for..." She pretended to think.

"About six minutes."

"Best six minutes of my life." He said it with utter sincerity. She'd come in like a tornado and turned his life upside down… and fixed everything that was wrong with it. She gave him back a hope that hadn't simply died—it had been obliterated. He didn't have words for the magnitude of the change she'd wrought in his life in just a few short days.

"The Colonel is officially under arrest," Piper said, totally switching subjects and dodging whatever she had been hiding before. "Daniel's bringing him up on charges."

"Fair enough. What's that got to do with why you're sitting in my lap but not letting me kiss you?" He wasn't going to let her off that easy.

"Just thought you might want to know." She ducked her head and went back to touching his scars. A frown etched on her face, which was ethereal in the moonlight, all shadows and sharp cheekbones and dark-as-midnight hair spilling over her shoulders. God, she was beautiful.

He brushed her hair back from where it had fallen across her face. The direct approach wasn't working, so he'd have to come at this sideways. "I'm glad to hear your brother is on Team Good Guys again."

She nodded. "He really is a straight arrow, but there's hope for him yet." Her smile was pained, and it was really starting to tear at him. "But the Colonel's slipperier than an eel. He's already talking *plea bargain*. And I wouldn't be surprised if someone up the chain of command gives it to him, just to keep his mouth shut."

Jace grimaced. That was all too likely. "No matter what, I'm not going to let him near you again."

She shook her head. "I'm not worried about that. I just want him to pay for what he's done. Unlike Agent Smith."

"Wait... what? What happened to Agent Smith?"

"Daniel says someone sprung him after about three hours. I think he must have some kind of connection to pretty high-level brass, maybe even Senator Krepky. As far as I know, he's still planning to propose that law about shifters—you know, the one where we all have to register? I'm sure the good Senator would be willing to pull some strings to keep Agent Smith out of the limelight and pin all of this on my father. Not that he's innocent, but one rogue Colonel is a whole different thing than the Feds being directly involved. He'll want to keep all that as quiet as possible when he goes for the new legislation."

"Well, that's easy, then," Jace said with a tight smile. "We don't keep quiet."

Piper nodded. "Olivia's already talking about taking the entire story to some guy in the press she knows. I guess she used to be a reporter or something?"

"Yeah. And that sounds like a reasonable approach." He ran his fingertips across her pale cheeks—she allowed it, but she wouldn't meet his gaze. She was still hiding something. He pressed on. "So, Olivia will take it to the press. Daniel will try to get your father to pay for what he's done. And Agent Smith might manage to slither under a rock. What's left?"

She took a deep breath, still avoiding his gaze. "Noah's going back overseas."

"I can imagine he'd like to get far away from here." Jace ducked his head and peered into her dark eyes, which were fixed on his chest. Was that it? Was she planning to go back to work overseas as well? Was that what she was hesitating to tell him?

The distant howl of his wolf welled up from deep inside him. It surged closer to the surface, but Jace was no longer afraid his beast would burst out at any moment. He and his wolf had just been reacquainted, and it felt good to be able to listen to what his wolf was telling him again. And right now, his wolf was insisting that Jace not let his mate go. Only Piper wasn't his mate—and she'd already made it very clear she never wanted one. Hot sex? Yes. Fall in love? Maybe. But a magical bond that forever tied her to him? No. And Jace could understand why—her father had abused everyone he loved, including his mate… who eventually killed herself to escape it. If all that had happened to him, Jace wasn't sure he would ever take the chance, either.

Piper was keeping silent, obviously struggling for words. He gave her time, not pushing.

Eventually, she said, "Daniel's going to stay here in Seattle at the Joint Base. Partly, I think, to make sure my father pays for what he did. Partly because Daniel's finally out from under his shadow—now he can have a career of his own. Taking down his own father and this horrible shifter experimentation program might even be what launches it."

"Good for Daniel." Jace waited, but it was clear he was going to have to force this out of her. "What about you?"

"What do you mean?" But he could tell by the way she was avoiding looking at him that she knew exactly what he meant.

Jace slid his hands up from her waist, along the soft length of her arms, and up to hold her cheeks gently by his fingertips. He tilted her face and brought her eyes up to meet his.

"I know you don't want to mate," he said softly. "And I get why. Your father has ruined so many lives, I'm sure you can't imagine mating as anything other than being horrifically trapped."

Her eyes were wide, and her lip trembled a little. It reminded him of when they made love, and how open and vulnerable she had been to him. His wolf responded to that sweetness and surged inside him, wanting to protect her from anything and everything that might hurt her. Including mating with him, if that was how it had to be.

"Having a mate..." He swallowed thickly, the words getting caught in his throat. "Well, it's not something I thought I would be able to have. But thanks to you, my wolf and I have a new understanding—one that doesn't involve him rampaging at night, out of control. And one where I listen to him, keep him close. As it should be. And right now, he's telling me to sink my fangs into you and claim you for my own."

Her lips parted, and he could feel her chest heaving.

He pushed one hand back through her hair and pulled her in for a quick kiss, soft and light and full of the tenderness he held in his heart for her.

Then he pulled back and continued, "It wasn't possible before, but now, I think I could—and I have you to thank for that. You've settled my wolf in a way he never was, even before what happened in Afghanistan. I have a faith in him that I didn't have before, now that I know the truth about what he did. What *we* did, together. But that doesn't change how you feel about mating—I understand that."

She shook her head in small rapid movements. "You *should* have a mate. It's not right for you to finally know the truth and not be able to reclaim everything an alpha like you should have."

He smiled. "I won't lie. Having a mate would be… *incredible.* Everything I've ever wanted. But it doesn't matter… all I want is you, Piper. You said before that you would stay—did you mean it?"

She visibly swallowed, and he didn't want to push her, but he was dying to know—was this just a three-day torrid affair like many she must have had before? He didn't think so, but he wasn't sure she wouldn't just walk away, now that her brother had been found. He needed to hear it straight from her lips, whatever the answer was going to be.

"Well, Seattle *is* a pretty city," she said, her voice trembling, "and there's plenty of counterintelligence work to do here—not least, I'd like to figure out what Krepky is really up to." She was changing the subject again.

And he wasn't going to let that happen. "I thought you liked traveling the world."

"I think, maybe, I've had enough of the world for a while." She touched him again, tracing her fingers from one scar to the next. She seemed to be searching for words, so he waited. "There's only one person my wolf has ever cried for," she whispered. "Only one she was ever willing to do *anything* for... including submit." She dragged her dark eyes up to meet his.

His heart swelled. "You would?" He held perfectly still, holding his breath, unsure he had even heard her right.

"Only for you." She bit her lip.

The joy welling up inside him was almost too much to contain. He let his hands slide to her shoulders and pulled her in for another kiss.

"Are you sure?" he gasped, his lips brushing hers. "If you do this, Piper, I promise—I'll never be anything like your father."

She smiled, her lips curving against his. "I know." She pulled back to look him in the eyes. "You're already a better man than anyone I know. And your wolf... goddammit, Jace, your wolf is fucking hot."

A bubble of laughter rose and burst out of him. "I'm fairly certain you're the only person who's ever thought that."

She looked askance at him. "I doubt that." She slid her arms around him and rose up in his lap, pressing her T-shirt clad chest against his bare one. "And if so, then everyone else is a complete idiot."

He gripped her hard, kissing her, barely believing she was actually doing this. Actually willing to do this. For him. *With him.*

He had to ask one more time. "Piper Wilding, I've never wanted anything so badly in this life as I've wanted to claim you as my mate. Please tell me you mean it. Please tell me that you believe me when I say I'll do everything in my power to love and protect you all the days of my life."

This time, there was no hesitation, just a smile. "Love is daring to be who you really are with someone. At least, that's how it should be. How I want it to be. And I want to take that dare with you."

His wolf growled in his need for her. Jace tipped her back on the bed so that she was lying on top of the blankets and his body was covering hers. "Goddammit, I want you so badly," he growled into her neck between hungry kisses. He really didn't need the words—his rock-hard cock was already pressing into her belly, explaining everything for him. What he needed was to remove all her clothing instantaneously.

"I like the sound of that," she whispered, holding his head and opening her neck more to his fervent tasting. But then she pushed him back and wriggled out from under him. She shifted to her wolf form as she went, rolling off the bed and landing on her paws in one smooth motion. She stood there, with her glistening black fur silver-tipped by the moonlight, eyes bright and shining for him. Then she stretched her paws forward, leaning back with her rump in the air and dipping her head.

*The submission pose.* She was submitting to him, and it charged his body with magic… and he wasn't even in wolf form yet, where it would be ten times more powerful. He brought his wolf out, and the magic surged inside him. The aches of the surgery and his wounds quickly faded, erased almost literally by her love.

He jumped down from the bed—his wolf form was so large that his ears had nearly been brushing the ceiling. He stood on all fours before her, tail erect, standing proud, striking the alpha pose that her submission automatically wrenched out of him.

*I pledge everything to you, my alpha.* Her thoughts made his heart soar, and then the magic of it rushed him—her magic had a wild feel to it, untamed and strong. He didn't need to ask—he knew she had never submitted to anyone voluntarily before. His wolf had always been strong, filled to the brim with magical power, but her submission supercharged him even further, literally strengthening him. He had submitted many times to his brother Jaxson, the lead alpha of the River pack, so he knew what it felt like on Piper's end of things—the rush of magic, the surge of power, wasn't something he drained from her. It was something they *shared*—each stronger for it. He could see the shine in her eyes grow brighter, her wolf's mouth dropping open and panting with the heat of it. He was desperate to claim her, right then and there—take her as his mate, claiming her with his bite and his love. But his hottest fantasies about claiming a mate hadn't taken place in his dingy bedroom.

This was the place where his wolf had thrashed and raged so many nights. They needed to go somewhere else. A special place for something as magical as this.

*Rise, my love.* He sent the thought to her, releasing her from the submission pose with words he never thought he would be able to say.

She leaped up and hurried over to him. His wolf was so large, she had to lift up on her hind legs to rub her muzzle against his. He dipped his massive head down and rubbed his face all over hers, along her body, covering her with his scent. He wanted to touch every part of her, and soon enough, he would do exactly that. Again and again, forever.

*Run with me, my love.* She yipped in response, and he led her out of his bedroom, charging down the stairs and rushing in a headlong chase through the kitchen that had him nipping at her as she playfully tried to catch him back.

Jace vaguely noticed there were other people in the house, milling around in the kitchen and the great room. They gasped in surprise as he and Piper raced past them, heading out into the night.

The others were unimportant.

The only thing that mattered to him was taking Piper

Wilding out to the forest that was his home, making mad love to her, and claiming her forever as his mate.

# CHAPTER 18

Piper raced to keep up with Jace's wolf.

Her paws pounded the hard-packed dirt outside the back kitchen door, but he was so big and strong and... *fast*. She could tell he wasn't even *trying* to race ahead, he just had to keep slowing down to stay close and loop back to nip playfully at her rump. They raced toward the forest outside the River family compound, and he was gorgeous in the moonlight–his thick, black fur shone with the magic of it. His wolf form radiated power, and as he turned back to her, she caught a glimpse of his giant-wolf-sized cock, hard and ready for her. A shudder ran through her—there was no way that thing could fit inside her, but she wouldn't mind running her tongue and hands along it. Her mouth watered just thinking about it—she wasn't joking when she said his wolf was *hot*. And that was *before* he had a monster erection. She suddenly got why Jace was so freaking well-endowed in his human form—it was a reflection of his wolf—and she couldn't wait to have him inside her again.

*Not much further,* Jace's thoughts came to her. He pulled ahead a little, leaping over fallen tree trunks that she could barely clear, his stride four times longer than hers. She struggled to keep up, but the power of the submission bond spurred her on.

She had been frankly terrified of submitting to him, but the bond turned out not to be a cage around her mind, the way she'd always envisioned it had trapped her mother. Submitting to Jace had lifted Piper **up.** Energized and empowered her in a way she never suspected was even possible. Her magic was strengthened, but even more—she felt adored. Protected. *Loved.* It was a literal feeling that enveloped her body, like a warm blanket wrapped around her tenderly and yet lifting her up. Rather than trapping her, submitting to

Jace had set her free.

Now she was even more eager for him to claim her—mating was supposed to be the pinnacle experience of every wolf's life. The best orgasm. The most intimate bond. The greatest love. All the things she'd heard for years, then cast off as ridiculous lies or simply something she would never have, suddenly became very real and very possible... and very much in the next few minutes. Her body thrummed with the excitement of it, and even in her wolf form, she was already wet for him. She'd never made love as a wolf—and with Jace's monster cock, it wasn't even possible—so she hoped they would quickly move on to the *human* part of the night's activities.

Piper caught up to Jace in a clearing in the forest. It was a flower-filled meadow of tall grasses, but all the flowers had closed up for the night, nudged into sleep by the moonlight. She met him in the middle of the wide open space and went up on her hind paws to nuzzle his face. She was desperate for him to shift back to human and plant that hot mouth of his on her... but first, there was something she wanted to do.

*Hold still,* she commanded, then she dropped back down to four paws.

*Hey, I'm the alpha here. I'm the one who's supposed to*— He cut off as she dived underneath his massive body and ran her tongue along the length of his monster-wolf cock. *Holy fuck*—

Then she couldn't hear his thoughts anymore because she had shifted human. She grabbed his cock with both hands—it was just that damn big—and now her human tongue was running across it. The growl that came from deep inside Jace's wolf was a rumble that vibrated through his cock and into her fingers. She stroked him and took him into her mouth. She could barely get the head to fit, with her jaws as wide as she could stretch them, but she devoured that tip like it was the most delicious and decadent lollipop she'd ever tasted.

Suddenly, he pulled away from her and shifted human. *"Jesus Christ, Piper!"* he panted, hands on knees, his erection still tall and bold in the moonlight. It was still enormous in human terms, but not the Mount Everest of Cocks she had in her hands and mouth a moment ago. "Are you trying to drive my wolf insane? Because I just got him under control." His voice was ragged.

She grinned mischievously and crawled across the grass on hands and knees toward him. They were both naked now, and she had every intention of making the most of that. "I just couldn't resist the temptation. I told you, your wolf makes me hot."

When she reached him, she planned on sliding his human cock deep into her throat, the way she hadn't been able to when he was wolfish and huge, but Jace pulled her up to standing before she could get hold of him.

"How the hell did I manage to land a Wilding?" he breathed. His face was equal parts amazed, horny, and adoring.

It melted Piper's heart. "You don't *land* one, you big, sexy beast. You *earn* one."

He pulled her close, crushing her chest to his and sandwiching his cock between them. Her nipples were hardened in the cool breeze of the night, and they pressed into the rigid muscles of his chest. His cock felt like a silky-hard piece of heaven held against her. His hands were running wild over her back, down to her rear end, up to her breasts… like he wanted to touch every inch of her skin. He kissed her briefly but fierce—and it sent a gush of wetness between her legs. She was *so* ready for him, she prayed he would take her soon. And hard. And again and again. If they spent the whole night in the meadow, she wouldn't complain.

He was breathing hard. "I don't know what I did to *earn* a Wilding, but I'll tell you this, Piper Wilding: I'm going to make you come so hard you scream my name. Then I'm going to bite my love into you."

"Yes. Please. Now."

He smirked, and that look made the muscles low in her belly clench tight. He had better *not* draw this out. She was too desperate to wait much longer.

"The submission," he breathed, one hand sneaking up to work her breast while the other found her bottom. "That turned me on so fucking hard." He slid his hand down between her legs and groaned. "God, Piper, you're already so wet for me."

Her hands clawed at his back, and she hiked her leg up over his hip to give him more access. "Stop teasing me, Jace River." She ground her hips against his. "I need you inside me."

But instead he moved his hand away from the touch she was craving. "Are you absolutely sure about this?" His breath was still ragged, but his voice had softened. "I can take you, pleasure you, give you more orgasms than you can count… but stop there. We could just make love, now, while the submission bond is at its height. But it will wear off eventually, at the next full moon. It's not permanent." His hand threaded into her hair and fisted, pulling her head back and exposing her neck to him. He bent to it, running the tip of his tongue along it, down to the crux where her neck and shoulder met. *"This* is where I'll mark you. *This* is permanent. This is everything I have to give to you, forever bound, forever loving you. But I want you to be absolutely, completely sure." He released his hold on her hair.

She moved her hands up from his shoulders to his face, holding him hard and staring deep into his eyes. "I am absolutely sure that if you don't fuck me right now, I might actually die from want. And if you don't claim me for your own, right here, tonight, sinking your fangs into my flesh and giving me everything you have, I'm going to die of a broken heart."

His eyes shone, and she didn't know if it was tears or if her own watery eyes were fooling her, but it didn't matter... because in the next instant, he gripped her bottom with both hands, hoisted her up, and then impaled her with his enormous cock. It went so deep and so hard, she shrieked.

Her head tipped back. "Oh, God, yes!"

He held her tight, standing upright in the meadow with her legs wrapped around him, and kept thrusting up into her with short bursts that shot her through with sparks of pleasure. Her climax was quickly building, and her panting rose with it. She clung to him, moving with him, meeting his every thrust with a downward stroke of her own. He was so big, filling her so completely, she felt like he was possessing her body outright, stretching both her body and soul with the power of his passion. Her orgasm rushed at her, unexpectedly, overtaking her so fast and hard, she screamed his name out into the night.

He groaned and slowed his pace, leaving her body and setting her down on her feet again. His cock glistened in the moonlight, slick with their lovemaking and engorged, even larger than before, if that was possible. She was light-headed, afraid that somehow he was done, but she wasn't thinking straight.

"Down on your knees." His voice was hoarse and heavy with need.

She dropped to her knees in front of him, eager to take him into her mouth, but she only got a taste before he fisted her hair, pulled her mouth away, and tilted her head up toward him towering over her.

"I am *so* going to have you do that later, my love," he panted. "*Fuck,* you are hot when you're sucking my cock."

She grinned up at him, and she could feel the shudder work through his body. His cock twitched and lightly brushed her lips. She reached her tongue out to lick it, and he groaned. Then he slowly moved behind her, still holding her hair to keep her in place. Then he pressed her forward, so that she had to drop down and brace her hands against the meadow grass.

"On your *hands* and knees," he said roughly. He was behind her, his cock already twitching against her rear end. With one hand in her hair, he slid the other between her legs, thrusting two fingers inside. She bucked against him.

"Jace, *please,*" she begged.

He pulled his fingers out, grabbed hold of her hip, and slammed his cock into her. She gasped and groaned at once, insanely glad to have him inside her again. His grip on her hair and her hip angled her just right so he could plunge deeper than she'd ever had him. His cock was so long and so thick, and he was driving so deep, that he was literally touching places inside her that no man ever had. Holding her firm, his thrusts grew stronger and harder. Her muscles quivered everywhere—between her legs, in her thighs, her breasts swinging hard with each pump he made—she thought sure she was about to crash into orgasm again.

"Fuck, Piper… you're so goddamn beautiful."

But she didn't need words from him, just the pounding of his cock, the feel of his hands… and then he bent over her, still thrusting, but slower, bringing his lips near her shoulder, right where it met her neck.

"You… are… mine," he panted, each word punctuated by a thrust.

"Yes!" she cried.

"Forever."

She could feel his fangs out, brushing her skin but not piercing.

"Take me!" Her voice was shrill, desperate, and hungry for him to *do it*. Claim her. Make her his.

The twin pricks of pain pushed her right over the edge. Her orgasm shuddered through her entire body, from the epicenter between her legs, straight up to her head and back to her toes, completely blowing the fuses in her mind in the process. Jace groaned and kept thrusting, and she could feel his hot seed spilling inside her. And the magic… his bite, which started out as the most pleasurable of pains, turned into a glowing white heat as his magic spread from where his mouth was clamped onto her. It pumped through her veins, filling her from the inside out, swimming electric white stars in front of her eyes. Her heart felt like it might burst straight out of her body, it was beating so wildly with the ecstasy. His love was working its way into every part of her, through and through, and she felt the tether, the magical bond that held them together. It was like the submission bond, only deeper and unbreakable and made of white-hot magic and love.

She *belonged* to him. *With* him. He was irrevocably part of her now—she would always carry his magic, a part of him inside her, even when he wasn't actively filling her with his cock and lavishing her with his love. He was home and family and love all bound into one being and one magical bond.

She had been running all this time—from shifters, from the shifting world, from the possibility of mating—and it suddenly dawned on her that this was exactly what she needed all along. This sense of *belonging* to someone. Jace was still inside her, slowing his movements, releasing his ardent hold on her body and her hair, and she had a flash of the future—small children that looked like *her* and *him*. Pups they would raise together. Their children would have their father's incredible strength and their mother's independence, and they would be surrounded by love all the days of their lives.

Jace pulled out of her with a delicious groan and fell back on the grass, pulling her down with him. She buried her head in his broad chest, but she couldn't stop the hot tears from cresting and sliding down her cheeks. His chest rose and fell, and she could hear the mad beating of his heart, but it wasn't long before he picked up his head to look at her.

He gently lifted her chin. "Why are you crying?" There was a tremor of fear in his voice, one she wanted to wipe away instantly… but she settled for grabbing his face and kissing him hard.

He was shocked and flushed and insanely in the moonlight. "Happy tears, my sexy beast. Just thinking about you and our future—that's enough to rip them out of me. I'll be okay in a minute."

A wide smile slowly grew on his face. "Our future?"

She propped herself up on his chest and stared down at him. "You know, the one where take me from behind, again and again, biting me with that insane magic high you're packing in those fangs. I mean, *damn,* Jace. You should have warned me mating was like this."

He chuckled and drew her closer. "You mean, you seriously didn't know?"

She snuggled into him. "Well, *sure*, I heard the stories. But there's a difference between the lewd gestures your friends make in high school and a screaming orgasm so out of this world that you see stars."

"Stars?" The laugh in his voice warmed her heart on top of the magic that was already there.

"Literal bright white shooting stars. I am not even kidding."

His fingers idly played along her back, then swept up to cup her breast. "I take it that means you liked it."

"Um…" She pretended to think about it. "Yes."

He grinned. "I'll have to work hard to top *literal shooting stars*. Probably need lots of practice." The joy on his face stole her breath.

"Lots and lots and *lots* of practice." The wind rustled the grass next to them, and she was quiet a moment, envisioning all the ways they would make love. All the places and positions and screaming orgasms that would fill their future. And then, one of those times, they would decide to let their love grow into something more—a child. Their love would create a little boy or a little girl, and that small one would be the embodiment of everything that was good in the world.

Jace touched her cheek, and she was surprised to see

his finger glisten with one of her tears.

His smile was replaced by a solemn look. "Thinking of our future again?"

She nodded, but she had to swallow down the tears before she could whisper, "A little girl, maybe. Or a boy. I don't care which."

His face opened in surprise, then he rolled over fast, taking her with him and pinning her against the grass. "Piper, I—" He choked up, paused a moment, then cleared his throat. "A daughter. I want a daughter."

The tears were coursing down her cheeks now, and she didn't bother to wipe them away, she just reached up to pull him down for a kiss. When they stopped again, she said, softly, "Then we'll have to keep trying until we have one."

A grin lit his face again, and it made her heart swell.

"You know…" he said. "Jaxson and Olivia are getting married soon. How about if we make it a double wedding?"

She struggled to shove the joy off her face and replace it with a serious look. "Absolutely not."

He frowned. "Please?"

She scowled at him. "I'm going to be busy making babies. No time for a wedding."

He laughed, hearty and whole, and it brought fresh tears to her eyes. "You're going to kill my mother with that kind of logic."

Piper rolled her eyes. "All right, then. A wedding. If we must."

He smiled wide then lowered his sights to her breasts. Her nipples were tight, reaching up to him, begging for his touch. His hooded eyes returned to hers. "Maybe I should make it up to you, having to tolerate this wedding business."

"Damn straight, you should." She was joking, of course, but she couldn't help the gasp when he dropped his mouth to her breast and started devouring her. Heat pooled between her legs, and her back arched as he pinched her other nipple. She didn't think she had another orgasm in her, but one had already started to build. And she should have known better...

With Jace River, anything was possible.

Want more River brothers?
JARED (River Pack Wolves 3)

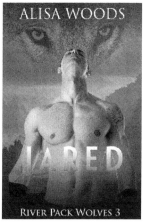

**He was broken by war.**
**Her secret could destroy her family.**
Get JARED today!

Subscribe to Alisa's newsletter to know when a new book
is coming out!
http://smarturl.it/AlphaLoversNews

# ABOUT THE AUTHOR

**Alisa Woods** lives in the Midwest with her husband and family, but her heart will always belong to the beaches and mountains where she grew up. She writes sexy paranormal romances about alpha men and the women who love them. She enjoys exploring the struggles we all have, where we resist—and succumb to—our most tempting vices as well as our greatest desires. She firmly believes that love triumphs over all.

All of Alisa's romances feature sexy alphas and the strong women who love them.

Printed in Poland
by Amazon Fulfillment
Poland Sp. z o.o., Wrocław